"It's only one date."

Kelly said it to herself. And if she felt any
doubt, it dissipated when she saw the tall,
lanky—handsome—cowboy lounging against
a lamppost outside the bar.

"Mr. Jefferson?"

He nodded, straightening to his full height.
"Hello," he said, his voice deep and stirring.
"Thanks for coming all the way out here."
Dark hair settled around his chin. His eyes
were shaded by his hat so that he looked
mysterious. And he gazed at her as if he'd
never seen a woman as beautiful.

Everything her mother had said about the wild,
charming Jefferson boys reverberated in Kelly's
ears. "I'm not the petite, cheery blonde you
requested," Kelly said, too quickly.

"No. You're not." A grin spread across his face.
"But I don't think I knew what I wanted."

ABOUT THE AUTHOR

Tina Leonard loves to laugh, which is one of the many reasons she loves writing Harlequin American Romance books. In another lifetime, Tina thought she would be single and an East Coast fashion buyer forever. The unexpected happened when Tina met Tim again after many years—she hadn't seen him since they'd attended school together from first through eighth grade. They married, and now Tina keeps a close eye on her school-age children's friends! Lisa and Dean keep their mother busy with soccer, gymnastics and horseback riding. They are proud of their mom's "kissy books" and eagerly help her any way they can. Tina hopes that readers will enjoy the love of family she writes about in her books. Recently a reviewer wrote, "Leonard has a wonderful sense of the ridiculous," which Tina loved so much she wants it for her epitaph. Right now, however, she's focusing on her wonderful life and writing a lot more romance!

Books by Tina Leonard

HARLEQUIN AMERICAN ROMANCE

748—COWBOY COOTCHIE-COO
758—DADDY'S LITTLE DARLINGS
771—THE MOST ELIGIBLE...DADDY
796—A MATCH MADE IN TEXAS
811—COWBOY BE MINE
829—SURPRISE! SURPRISE!
846—SPECIAL ORDER GROOM
873—HIS ARRANGED MARRIAGE
905—QUADRUPLETS ON THE DOORSTEP
977—FRISCO JOE'S FIANCÉE†
981—LAREDO'S SASSY SWEETHEART†
986—RANGER'S WILD WOMAN†
989—TEX TIMES TEN†
1018—FANNIN'S FLAME†

HARLEQUIN INTRIGUE

576—A MAN OF HONOR

†Cowboys by the Dozen

FANNIN'S FLAME
Tina Leonard

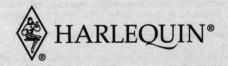

TORONTO • NEW YORK • LONDON
AMSTERDAM • PARIS • SYDNEY • HAMBURG
STOCKHOLM • ATHENS • TOKYO • MILAN • MADRID
PRAGUE • WARSAW • BUDAPEST • AUCKLAND

ISBN 0-373-75022-6

FANNIN'S FLAME

Copyright © 2004 by Tina Leonard.

www.eHarlequin.com

Printed in U.S.A.

THE JEFFERSON BROTHERS
OF MALFUNCTION JUNCTION

Mason (37)—He valiantly keeps the ranch and the family together.

Frisco Joe (36)—Newly married, he lives in Texas wine country with his wife and daughter.

Fannin (35)—Should he pack up and head out to find their long-lost father, Maverick? Or search for that perfect woman?

Laredo (34), twin to Tex—His one passion was to go east and do Something Big, which meant marrying the love of his life and moving to North Carolina.

Tex (34), twin to Laredo—Determined to prove he's settled, he left his rose garden for the good girl who captured his heart.

Calhoun (33)—He's been thinking of hitting the rodeo circuit.

Ranger (32), twin to Archer—He gave up on joining the military to join his new wife in their RV.

Archer (32), twin to Ranger—He'll do anything to keep his mind off his brothers' restlessness—even write poetry to his lady pen pal in Australia.

Crockett (30), twin to Navarro—He's an artist who loves to paint portraits—of nudes.

Navarro (30), twin to Crockett—He may join Calhoun in the bull-riding game.

Bandera (26)—He spouts poetry like Whitman—and sometimes nonsense.

Last (25)—Never least, he loves to dispense advice, especially to his brothers.

To Maria Velazquez and her little Joy—
Maria, thanks for the inspiration.

Lisa and Dean—
all mothers should be so blessed. Kimmie, all sisters
should be so blessed. I love you. Fred Kalberer—
thank you for taking care of me and Mom.

Many thanks to Harlequin and all the wonderful
people there who make Tina Leonard who she is.
Stacy, five down—yeehaw!

And many thanks to the readers who like their men
a little on the rascally side—
your loyal encouragement means so much.

Chapter One

If music tames the savage beast, then your
mother was a full orchestra accompanied by a
choir of angels.
—Maverick Jefferson to his sons one winter
night when the loneliness became too much

"What I'm saying is feel the romance, Princess,"
Fannin said. "Smell the breeze. Hear the sigh of the
grass. Rejoice in the call of the wild. Entice that bull,
Princess, please," he pleaded with his cow to the
delight of his three brothers.

"Could you turn it up, Romeo?" Archer asked. "I
don't think the people of Union Junction have heard
you spout such poetry in all the years you've lived
here."

"Do you have to do it this way?" Calhoun com-
plained. "Can't you be normal and use a syringe to
get a calf in her?"

"Hey!" Fannin said with a frown. "I know it's not

logical. But I want Princess to conceive the natural way.''

''Or no way at all,'' Navarro said. ''I see no interest on the part of her suitor.''

Indeed, the bull, Bloodthirsty Black, usually such a firebringer of hell and mortification upon hapless cowboys, appeared uninterested in his bride.

''Why don't you tell Bloodthirsty how it's done, Fannin?'' Archer asked, gasping with smothered laughter. ''After all, you *are* the expert with women.''

Fannin grimaced as his brothers slapped each other on the backs. ''I sort of have a date Saturday night,'' he said, not totally lying.

''A date!'' They all leaned forward from their posts on the fence. ''Who's the lucky girl?''

Fannin turned away so they couldn't see his face. ''I'm taking Helga to the movies. She wants to see a movie in Dallas. And I think it's time our housekeeper got off the ranch for a few hours. You dopes haven't noticed, but Helga's homesick for Germany. She's lonely. So I'm taking her out.''

''Helga!'' They roared with laughter.

Navarro grinned. ''Yeah, I'd like to go out with a battle-ax. That'd be *my* choice of female companionship.''

''That's not very nice,'' Fannin said with a frown. ''She's been working hard to take care of us. You know, you ought to think about taking her out yourselves. Helga doesn't work at our ranch just to put up with your majestic egos.''

They stared at him.

"All I ever go out with is twins," Fannin mimicked in a high voice. "Did you see that pair of twins on Rosie Mayflower?" That was exactly how his brothers would talk—and did talk—about women.

"Now, those are some twins," Archer agreed. "Navarro, does Rosie have any cousins with the same genetic traits? There has to be some family relations she could introduce us to."

"Breasts aren't everything," Fannin pointed out.

"But they are something," Navarro said, "and they count big-time in my book."

"Anyway," Archer said, "you're not even talking to Princess right, Fannin. A woman doesn't want to be begged or pleaded with for sex. She wants to be told how it's going to be. She wants to be ravaged. Stormed and conquered. If she knows what the game is up-front, then she's happy to play. No wonder you don't have any real dates."

"Well, it is true that the early caveman didn't have any trouble getting a woman," Fannin said. "He just dragged her off by the hair."

"No point in getting rough," Calhoun said. "All we're suggesting is that your way is too subtle to get a woman's attention. Notice we get the women, while you tend to get the sister with the good personality and the insurmountable chastity."

"Because I don't storm the gates," Fannin finished.

"Afraid he's right," Navarro said. "Never let a

woman have the upper hand, especially in the sack, or you'll wind up with a Helga running your world. In other words, you'll end up whipped when you should be putting your feet up after a long day, with a very attractive female ready to bring you a beer, serve you your supper in a comfy armchair and then put you to bed with a smile on her face.''

"That's what I mean," Fannin said sadly to Princess. "My brothers are all so artificial. They only think of one thing. Don't worry about that stupid bull not wanting you," he told his favorite cow. "He's probably lost all his good genes throwing cowboys around."

"Princess is not a pet," Calhoun said sternly.

"She is to me. And I want a good calf out of her. I'm giving a calf to Mimi's baby when it's born, so her little girl will have money in the bank when she grows up."

"And the calf can't come from a syringe," Navarro said, shaking his head.

"The best things take time," Fannin said briskly. "And the right moment. Magic."

"And I say you're going to be waiting a helluva long time, you and your Princess." Archer slapped his hat against his leg and hopped off the rail. "I got work to do."

His other brothers murmured something similar, leaving Fannin alone with Princess and her lackluster lover.

"Hey," he said to the bull, "you're supposed to

be the hottest thing on hooves. What's your problem? I had to haul you out here in a special trailer so you wouldn't do damage to yourself. Half the county said I was crazed to even let you near Princess. They said, do it the right way, but I said no, natural was better. And look at you over there. You couldn't care less. I believe you're only good for the ring, you old show pony.''

Fannin sighed, his brothers' words eating at him. It was true he didn't date much. He didn't have the ruthlessness in him to love and leave a woman. He had to admit, his brothers' techniques did seem to drive the women wild. Truthfully, Fannin thought, he had some things in common with Bloodthirsty Black.

Last year had seen enough settling down to suit all the Jefferson brothers—four brothers down but eight determined not to make a trip to the altar. Fannin was in no hurry to get into a relationship.

''But I would like a date,'' Fannin told Princess. ''Not counting the one with Helga. Actually, I want a night of rowdy sex. Lusty fornication. With the right woman, though.'' He looked at Princess. ''Unfortunately, to get the right woman I'd have to order up. Made-to-order, like Bloodthirsty is for you. All the best genes. I could say, okay, this is what I want, and I want her to do this and not to do that, and I don't want any flak about it. Then my brothers would have to shut up. But how do I get that?''

Princess ignored him.

''My brothers say their blue-ribbon goal is sex in

the morning, every morning, and it'd be a best-case scenario if they could relieve themselves without having to worry about the woman. Who cares if she climaxes? And please get out of the bed quickly and quietly. Vamoose!'' He sighed with frustration. ''They're such syringe types.''

The only time a woman had come to the ranch without designs on any of the brothers it had been an accident. Actually, it had been *women* who'd arrived, courtesy of an e-mail that his eldest brother, Mason, and their next-door neighbor, Mimi, had missent. All hell had broken loose when the females from Lonely Hearts Station had arrived.

But so many good things had come out of that stray e-mail, from weddings to babies.

And even Helga. Mimi had called her friend, Julia Finehurst, of the Honey-Do Agency and asked for a female housekeeper, one that Mason couldn't fall in love with, even though Mimi knew she'd never have Mason. Mimi was just that way about keeping Mason pinned in a corner.

Helga had arrived, and Fannin could honestly say the square, stout German housekeeper kept all the brothers in line. Like a female military sergeant. Mimi had played the prank of all pranks on Mason.

Fannin wouldn't want to date anyone as fiery as Mimi. A woman like that would probably blow the flame out of him eventually. He wanted a woman, but he wanted the *right* woman—for now. For a night or two. Maybe even a month. No tricks. No drama. Plenty of sex. Was it so much to ask?

Fannin's mother had been calm, loving and content to live on a faraway ranch with twelve boys and a loud rascal husband who was popular among the townspeople—the ladies. They'd all known who ruled the Jefferson roost with quiet, admirable control. Maverick Jefferson was never happier than when his wife had him wrapped securely around her little finger.

Fannin groaned. They just didn't make women like that anymore. And maybe his brothers were right. His technique had to go or he was going to end up alone, living at the ranch with Mason and his other fathead brothers. Today's women seemed to require more machismo out of a man, and he'd call himself a John Wayne type rather than a jerk in cowboy gear. But if that's what today's woman needed, he supposed he could force a little more chauvinism into his approach.

"Good night," he said to the bounty bull. "I doubt you'll get matters figured out, but I'll leave you here awhile just in case. And you, Miss Princess, you just try to be a docile lass if your man comes a-courting."

Fannin headed up to the house and went into Mason's office. Reaching into the haphazard Rolodex, he pulled out a card for the Honey-Do Agency. He sat down at the computer and typed in the e-mail address. He'd heard the agency was branching out into matchmaking services. They probably didn't have dream women in their database, and he was feeling a little nervous about telling them exactly what he wanted in a one-night companion. He read over the card again. ''I'll say I want to interview a personal assistant for one night to accompany me on a possible business trip.''

He began to state his needs. ''Attractive, understanding, somewhat petite female,'' he typed happily. ''For a big-hearted cowboy who needs a special companion. She needs to have a good sense of humor, too.''

It sounded like a personals ad. They weren't going to be fooled. It also sounded like he was looking for an artificial female.

''Okay, let's try the truth. I want an easygoing woman,'' he typed. ''Easygoing is *key*.''

''That's my problem,'' he said with a sigh. ''I'm always worrying about being heavy-handed. My brothers would just fire this puppy off and never think twice about sounding like tree dwellers.''

Well, Tarzan he wasn't, but he wanted a Jane for one night. A Jane he'd practically designed himself. ''There are bigger sins on the planet than being a male chauvinist. Here goes nothing,'' he said and hit the Send key.

IN JULIA FINEHURST'S office at the Honey-Do Agency, Kelly Stone was in charge while her boss was sick. She'd just logged the final client and picked up her extralarge purse to leave for the weekend when she remembered she hadn't turned off the computer.

She bent to click the screen closed and saw that a new e-mail had popped up. The Jefferson Union Junction ranch return address caught her eye, and she opened the message. Kelly got a lot of news from her mother, Helga, whenever Julia wrote to check on her employee.

"My name is Fannin Jefferson," Kelly read. "I need a personal assistant for one evening."

She laughed. "Oh, that's a new one. Why don't you just say you need a date?"

She seated herself in the chair to read the rest of the request. From everything her mother had told her, the wild boys of Malfunction Junction did not have to go hunting for women. Women knocked those boys over any chance they could. Her mother had mentioned thongs in the mailbox and bras hanging off the front doorknob, all inscribed with phone numbers, names or addresses.

"Attractive, understanding, somewhat petite female," she read. "Mr. Jefferson, you are obviously way too proud of yourself. You want to order the moon to spec, and say it's a *job*. Then you can fire my employee when she doesn't meet your lofty requirements."

No one would describe Kelly as attractive or petite. She had her mother's German genes, which showed in her robustness, and her Irish father's red hair, neither of which brought men running to her side.

"Needs to have a good sense of humor," she read out loud. Blinking, she thought about all the women the agency had on file: mothers, secretaries, teachers, even a mathematician. It wouldn't be hard to find someone dainty for him, even though the agency's matchmaking file was small. Yet it wouldn't be fair to send the women out on a false lead to a persnickety, overimpressed-with-himself cowboy who maybe had no intention of being any nicer to his "assistant" than he was to Kelly's mother.

"Mr. Smooth Operator," she murmured. "Ordering Dream Date Barbie so you can send her back after you've looked under her skirt. No, I don't think so, Lascivious Ken."

Maybe Kelly would go there herself.

She knew her mother was homesick. She had been worried enough to threaten to come visit the ranch and slap those wily cowboys into line herself if they didn't start appreciating Helga. It hurt Kelly's feelings that her mother was sad, especially during the Christmas season. A job was a job, but her mother had been at the Jefferson household for nearly a year now.

"My mother has a heart of gold," Kelly said, peering into her oversize purse. "Those cowpokes ought to know that by now. Obviously, they're not too bright. Isn't that right, Joy?"

Kelly pulled out her very red, very opinionated teacup poodle, a sweet baby who had bonded with Kelly instantly upon the dog's rescue from the local animal shelter.

"Miss Joy," Kelly said, "what do you think about a road trip to visit Grandma?"

Joy quivered in her hands. Kelly adjusted the poodle's little sweater and fake-diamond collar as she thought about Fannin's request.

"It's only one night," Kelly said to the poodle. "There's nothing on our dance card for tonight or tomorrow. Mama's homesick, and we can cheer her up. And it wouldn't hurt this ornery cowboy too much if his order isn't exactly fit-to-fill. We just won't charge him while we teach him to mind his manners better where your grandma is concerned. Or better yet, we could *double bill* him! He'd deserve it, the rat, even though Julia wouldn't allow it."

Joy licked Kelly's hand. No crime was being committed if every tiny detail wasn't perfect for Fannin Jefferson.

Kelly reread the e-mail. "Good sense of humor," she repeated, switching off the computer and getting up from the chair. She turned out the lights. "Gee, cowboy, hope you don't mind a little joke being played on *you.*"

"I'VE THOUGHT OF A WAY to get rid of Helga," Archer said smoothly. "This is so easy we should have thought of it before."

"Mason likes her. At least she keeps him reasonably happy. For years, we've dreamed of him getting off our cases. What's the point of changing a good thing?" Calhoun asked.

"We could have a new housekeeper. We could talk one of the Union Junction Salon girls into coming over here to work for us," Navarro said reasonably.

"Yeah," Bandera agreed, flipping some cards onto the table. "Give me an ace out of the deck, Last."

"May I just point out that whatever you do to Helga will adversely affect Mimi," Last said. The youngest brother, he was prone to clear thinking at times and steering his brothers on *many* occasions. "Mimi needs help with her dad. The sheriff hasn't improved in months."

"Mimi's happily pregnant," Crockett pointed out. "I mean, have you seen the size of her lately? She looks like she swallowed the Great Pumpkin. Marriage clearly agrees with her."

"I dunno," Last said. "I don't think she's all that happy."

The brothers stared at him.

"Then let Mimi hire Helga, since Mimi hired Helga for us in the first place," Archer said, annoyed. "That's the proper thing to do, and it was what I was going to suggest. Mimi needs Helga more than we do. Mimi sneakily hired Helga in here to keep Mason occupied. But now Mimi's married, so Mason is free to shake loose of those shackles. I say this is the right solution for everyone. And I want to get up in the morning and look at a face that's young and beautiful and smiling. Instead of scouring me."

"Scouring you?" Bandera asked. "Do you mean souring you?"

"No. I mean scouring me. I put my elbows on the table and she scours me with her eyes. I put my feet on the coffee table, she scours me. I leave clothes lying on the floor in my room, and she scours me. It's like being assaulted daily by a Brillo pad."

"She doesn't have to clean our houses, just Mason's," Calhoun pointed out. "She doesn't have to take care of anyone except Mason, since he's really the one who wants her."

"Archer has a good theory," Last said slowly. "I never thought of it before, but with four less of us on the ranch, we don't need as much help as we did. Mimi's got her sick dad and a baby on the way. We could offer Helga's services to the Cannadys."

Archer sighed with relief. "I just knew you'd see it my way."

Fannin walked in, tossing his hat on the table.

"Any luck?" Last asked him. "Call out the harpist yet to serenade the hooved lovers with romantic music?"

"Shut up," Fannin demanded.

"We've got a plan we need your vote on, ornery one," Bandera said. "How would you feel about us giving Helga to Mimi as a baby gift?"

Fannin grinned. "Now that's the first positive thing y'all have said all day. The sooner the better!"

He fixed himself some lunch, feeling much better about life in general. The phone rang in the kitchen. "Fannin Jefferson," he said.

A soft voice said, "Mr. Jefferson? This is the

Honey-Do Agency calling to confirm and fill your order.''

He scrambled with the phone, the sandwich he'd fixed and a notepad into the farthest corner of the kitchen so his nosy brothers couldn't hear. The minute they realized he was trying to have a private conversation, they grouped around him, listening.

''Do you mind?'' he demanded of them.

''Mr. Jefferson?'' the voice asked.

He couldn't help noticing that the voice was sweet. But confident. ''Just a moment, please. I'm having some interference here.''

''I'm on a cell phone,'' the sweet voice said. ''I'm afraid the line is breaking up. Can you meet your date in town, to help her get to the ranch?''

''Absolutely,'' he said. ''How about we meet at Lampy's Bar on the square?''

''I'll tell her,'' the voice said. ''Nine o'clock all right?''

''It's fine.'' He shooed his brothers away. ''Um, does that mean that tonight is the one night she's going to be my personal companion?''

''Well, no, Mr. Jefferson,'' the voice said with a laugh. ''You can keep her as long as you need to, if you accept her,'' the woman said. ''This is just an interview, is it not? Since your needs were pretty specific.''

He recognized he was being teased and wasn't sure what to think about it. The woman's voice was giving him a strange buzz, almost as if she were blowing kisses into his ear.

"Normally, billing would begin in the morning, at eight o'clock. However, we feel it's important that your assistant finds you to her liking, as well. You understand."

There was that subtle laughter in her voice again. Fannin turned to face the kitchen wall so that his brothers couldn't read his expression. "It's business, not pleasure," he stated, lying through his teeth but not wanting to seem like a man who needed to call up for a private companion. Damn, but this was getting complicated. He'd have to find her some typing to do.

Why did I let my brothers goad me into dialing up a date?

"Goodbye," the voice said, and the line went dead.

"Oh crap!" Fannin said to himself. "I forgot all about my date tonight!"

"You have a date?" Last asked quickly.

"The Helga date. Remember? I promised to take her into Dallas." Rattled by getting a callback from the agency so quickly, he'd forgotten about Helga. "What plans do you have tonight?" he asked his brothers.

They shifted uncomfortably.

"You know, since you're plotting to get rid of her, this ought to make you feel better," Fannin said. "Be nice to her before you boot her."

"You don't like her, either," Last said.

"No," Fannin agreed. "I don't think that's a reason to plot her unemployment, though." He sighed. "However, I'm putting my vote in with this plan just because I do think she'd be happier taking care of a baby, the sheriff and Mimi than you ungrateful lot. Who's going to tell Mason what you're up to?"

Archer stood. "You are?"

"Me? Why would I? I didn't hatch this scheme." He wasn't going to have any part of telling Mason that the one person who made him happy was going to have to find new digs next door.

Crockett kicked back in the chair, balancing it on its legs. "If you want us to take Helga out tonight so that you can go wherever it is you're going, we think it's only fair you talk to Mason."

They had a point, even if it was blackmail. Fannin pursed his lips. The lady on the phone had sounded so sexy. Of course, that wasn't his date, but if his date was anything like the bearer of that voice…his ears would be the happiest part of his body.

At least until he could talk her out of her clothes.

"Deal," he said reluctantly. "You butt-heads."

The brothers slapped each other's hands while Fannin looked on sourly.

"Freedom, here we come!" Navarro yelled.

"Ding-dong, the witch is dead!" Bandera howled.

Annoyed, Fannin left the room, comforting himself with the thought that he'd soon be at Lampy's Bar meeting his dream date. Picked just for him, by the sexy-sounding secretary.

He just wished he didn't feel like such a Judas.

Chapter Two

If Kelly felt any remorse over deceiving Fannin Jefferson, it dissipated immediately when she saw the tall, lanky cowboy lounging against a lamppost outside Lampy's Bar. "Mr. Jefferson?"

He nodded, straightening to his full height, which Kelly was gratified to note was taller than her full height. She was no small, delicate thing, standing nearly six feet without the small, stacked heels on the winter boots she was wearing. "I'm Kelly Stone," she said. "Your personal assistant."

She saw hesitation in his gaze—then realized that hesitation had turned to something else as he took her hand.

"Hello," he said, his voice deep and stirring. "Thanks for coming all the way out here."

Oh, she didn't want to be attracted to him. But his hand warmed her chilled fingers and his voice settled her nerves. This big man carried security in every inch of his frame, and she responded to it like a lost calf.

"I'm not the petite, cheery blonde you ordered. That was what you requested, wasn't it?" Kelly asked, her words speeding as he let go of her hand.

A grin spread across his face. "No. You're not what I ordered. But I don't think I knew what I wanted."

She stared at him. He was tall, dark, handsome. So cliché. Candy for females. Dark hair settled around his chin. Didn't the man believe in haircuts? She couldn't see whether he had a bald spot hiding under his hat, but she doubted it. The man had too much confidence to be hiding any flaws. His chin was firm and strong, his lips full and sensual. She liked his lips best, if she ignored that his chest was as wide as Ohio. His eyes were shaded enough by the hat so that he looked mysterious. Marlboro man come to life, except he stood in the misty night as if he'd never seen a woman as beautiful as she.

Everything her mother had said about the wild Jefferson boys reverberated in her ears. Yet her body was responding in the strangest way to this man. Didn't mother always know best? Helga wouldn't want her daughter getting a crush on a Jefferson male. She would warn Kelly that nothing good could come of it. "I suppose you're perfectly horrid," Kelly said, "or else you wouldn't have to order a personal companion. There must be lots of ladies in this town who would be willing to 'work' for you."

He winked at her. "Yeah."

"Yeah what? You're horrid or lots of ladies applied for the job? When do you fill me in on my supposed duties?''

He laughed, taking her arm. ''Come on. You look cold.''

A small bark reminded Kelly of her manners. ''I'm sorry,'' she told the cowboy. ''This is Joy.'' She took the small red poodle out of her bag, holding Joy up so that Fannin could see her. ''Do you think Mr. Lampy will mind a dog in his bar?''

Fannin took Joy from her, slipping the tiny dog inside his jacket. ''Now he won't.''

Kelly hesitated, shocked that Joy had gone so willingly. Her spoiled and opinionated baby didn't like anyone. Even more surprising, the cowboy wasn't irritated that she'd brought a pet. Suddenly she felt guilty that she hadn't been honest with him about who she was. She should tell him. Certainly this brother couldn't have been disrespectful of her mother's feelings.

Then again, Helga had said the Jeffersons were an extraordinarily charming lot.

That didn't change the reality, either, that as soon as Fannin found out she was Helga's daughter, the pumpkin coach was going to leave the curb. But Fannin was staring at her like she was something special, someone attractive and meaningful whose company he was enjoying. And that wasn't a feeling a six-foot redhead usually got from a man.

Dishonesty was going to have to work for just a

while longer. A little more starry glow—before she had to put away the fairy-tale props.

"Everything all right?" Fannin asked. "You look like something's not good."

"Everything is good," Kelly replied quietly.

Too good.

FANNIN WAS HAVING a hard time not staring at the statuesque redhead as she tossed a dart with strength and accuracy toward the wall target. "There you go," he said. "You can't do any better than that."

She sipped her wine and nodded. "Pretty good for never having thrown darts before."

"How old are you?" Fannin asked. He had to know. She seemed so fresh and young and cheerful.

"Thirty. You?"

"Thirty-six now. Had a birthday."

"Happy one?"

"Yeah. Our housekeeper baked me a cake. It was nice. No one's done birthday cakes in our house in years."

Her brows rose. "That was nice of your house-keeper."

He nodded. "German chocolate cake, even, from scratch. Old family recipe. It was wonderful."

Kelly's eyes widened. "Did she know you liked it?"

He thought that was an odd question but skipped it. "Of course. She tries hard." He hoped Helga was having fun in Dallas and that his dunderhead brothers were being kind to her. "Another wine?"

"No, thanks. If you don't mind, it was a long drive and—"

"Of course," he said hastily. Why had he kept her out so late? This wasn't a date. Well, it sort of was, secretly, but she was a professional, a working woman who was on the clock at eight in the morning. Dang! He still needed to think of a job for her to do.

How was he going to get her to go out with him again? This was probably the type of woman who would say she didn't mix business with pleasure, so he'd probably screwed himself royally.

"I don't mean to be rude," Kelly said to him, "but I never mix business with pleasure. And I'm having way too much fun tonight. You know?"

He stared at her. His brothers were wrong; he hadn't lost his touch with women! He just needed the right one. Or *a* right one. Problem was the business and pleasure comment. If he fired Kelly tonight, would she go out with him tomorrow night?

Probably a very bad idea. "Come on," he said. "Let me take you home to bed."

She looked at him patiently, her eyes large and dark in the dim bar, and he hoped she could overlook his major Freudian slip.

"I meant, let me take you home so you can get to bed."

She nodded. "I knew what you meant."

"Good," he said, chuckling nervously. "Because I wouldn't want you to think I mean—"

"You were very clear about what you wanted," Kelly reminded him. "A personal companion. Petite. Sense of humor. Nothing like me. So I feel safe with you."

Guess again, Little Red Riding Hood, he thought. That voice of hers drove him nuts. He wanted to go to sleep with that voice whispering to him; he wanted to hear her— "Hey, you called the house earlier, didn't you?"

She hesitated, then nodded.

"Why didn't you tell me you were coming out for the job?"

"I don't know." Her gaze dropped for a second. "I guess I wouldn't have come out if you'd sounded like a horse's ass."

"Why would I be a horse's ass?"

She shrugged.

"You're not a man-hater, are you? One of those crazy females who think all men are scum?" His brothers' advice came to mind, floating eerily in his memory. He was too easy, too kind, too gentle. He usually got left with empty sheets while his brothers set beds afire.

Kelly's glance slid away from him. He checked her fingers. No rings. But the poodle shifted in his jacket, snuggling closer to his warmth. Would an unmarried woman come all the way out here for one day's worth of employment? He frowned. Something wasn't right here.

"I don't hate men," she said. "I'm just careful around…men I don't know."

That sounded plausible, even prudent. Still, unease washed away the former comfort he'd felt with Kelly. She could be blowing him off—killing him with professional kindness. "I suppose the agency wouldn't have sent you out here if they felt like we mistreated our employees. We've had one employee for a year, and she's happy enough."

Kelly blinked at him.

"Are you afraid of me?" he asked.

"Not exactly. Not afraid. Really, caution's just my nature."

"Well, have you decided whether or not I'm a horse's ass?" he asked. "Because you don't have to come to the ranch if you don't feel secure."

"A job's a job," she said.

He squinted at her. Last would know which way the wind was blowing for this woman. His brothers would give her little attention and make her hungry by starvation.

One minute she'd seemed very warm for him. The next, cool as the weather outside.

She was just his type, even if he'd never known he preferred Amazonian redheads. In fact, she was steaming the creases right out of his jeans. He didn't want her to lose interest in him.

Princess had ignored Bloodthirsty Black—and vice

versa. No Pow! At least at first sight. His brothers
understood Pow!

It was time to change his ways. "C'mon," he said
gruffly. "You've got a hard day's work ahead of you
tomorrow. You're going to need all the rest you can
get."

He was rewarded by a flash of disappointment on
Kelly's face. Then she nodded. Directing her toward
his truck, he said, "You'll be able to follow me easily, even though it's dark. I'll drive slow. We'll be at
the ranch in about twenty minutes. Pay close attention
to the road markings, so that when you leave tomorrow night, you'll remember your way."

There. Business totally unmixed from pleasure.

He had her on the run. His brothers would be
proud.

KELLY WISHED SHE didn't feel so guilty! Fannin was
so much more man than she'd expected him to be—
and he was making her nervous. False pretenses were
obviously not her game. She sighed, watching the
truck ahead carefully. Fannin was a careful driver,
and he seemed equally careful with his heart. What
had possessed her to say that he might be a horse's
ass? The moment she had, he'd gone distant on her.
She hated that! She was always sticking her size-ten
shoe in her mouth.

Then she'd had to fall back on the professional
excuse, so it wouldn't seem like she'd been chasing
him when all he wanted from her was a day's worth

of work. What had gotten into her to stand there drooling like a madwoman? If her mouth hadn't run off with her chances, she would have been in danger of losing all self-respect and throwing herself at that poor unsuspecting man.

Wouldn't he have been surprised to find her wrapped around him like a well-worn sweater? "Maybe all he really wants is a secretary, Kelly. You *assumed* he wanted a date, even though he never asked for a date. You thought he was going to make a move on you, and when he didn't, your sex signals tripped a major breaker. You need to settle down and be professional, be a good representative of Julia's Honey-Do Agency."

Joy had certainly not carried any inhibitions. Her baby was still in Fannin's jacket, nice and warm and secure. Of course, things were a lot less complicated in the animal world. Dogs didn't bog themselves down with overthought. They looked for love and comfort, and they got it where they could. "Of course, I can't exactly fit into his pocket," Kelly murmured. Nor his life.

Then she noticed he was stopping up ahead, suddenly. She thought she had the steering wheel firmly in her hands, but she must have been trembling. The car went over something hard and bumpy in the road, something large, and the steering wheel jerked from her fingers. Gasping, she overcompensated and slid into the ditch. "Oh, for heaven's sake!" Mentally, she checked for broken anything—everything felt fine. Except her pride, of course, as Fannin's truck door slammed on the embankment above her.

"You all right?" he called.

Not if you count my humiliation level. "I'm fine," she called back.

"Anything hurt?" Fannin slid on his feet toward the car and opened her door to gingerly help her out. "Move slowly. Make sure everything's in one piece."

"I'm fine," she said weakly, becoming more unsettled now that the adrenaline was wearing off. "I hit something."

"A deer."

"A deer! I didn't see a deer."

"It's lying on its side in the road. Probably was meandering across when someone accidentally hit it. That happens around here sometimes. You're lucky it was just a small one."

She shuddered. "How come you didn't hit it?"

"I saw it, but my truck's set up higher than your car. I didn't have time to warn you."

His fingers felt good as they massaged her neck, her shoulders, her arms, checking her over and steadying her. "I'm fine, really. It was my own stupidity. My mind was a million miles away. I saw you stop, but my reaction was slow."

"You wouldn't have been expecting a deer in the road," he said kindly.

All she wanted to do was melt into his arms. "Where's Joy?"

"I left her up in the truck. She'd made a nest in my jacket and was perfectly happy not to come back out into the cold. Are you sure you're fine?"

Looking up at him, she said, "Well, having never hit a deer before, I think I'm woozy."

He frowned. "Woozy?"

"Yeah. Isn't that funny? I feel light-headed."

"Maybe you have a concussion."

She could hear the instant worry in his voice. "No," she said slowly, "I didn't hit my head. I think I'm just envisioning poor Bambi—"

"Hey." He took her into his arms and held her close. "Don't think about it, okay? The deer was dead and didn't feel a thing. You didn't hurt the deer. In fact, I heard a rumor that it was an evil deer, out looking for little forest creatures to lure from their warm, snug homes. You did the world a favor. Okay?"

"Evil deer?" But she giggled, in spite of herself. "Thanks. I'm feeling better now." More from his chest and his solid warmth than his silliness, but that felt good, too.

"Good. We're going to leave your car here, until I can come back with my brothers so they can help me tow it back up this embankment."

"Oh, no. I don't want you to go to the trouble. I'll call a service."

He laughed, and she loved the sound of it coming from deep in his chest.

"We *are* the service in this town. Didn't you see the size of my truck?"

"I hadn't looked." She'd only been looking at him.

"Other people buy bling-bling. We bought the biggest trucks they had on the market. Therefore, we became the towing service by default. We even pulled Shoeshine Johnson's bus out of the pond when it slipped in."

"How does a bus slip into a pond?" This man was telling her whoppers just to get her to calm down, and it was working better than wine.

"That's a story for another time. Come on. I need to get you warm. Easy up the hill," he said, more carrying her than letting her walk.

"I'm fine, Fannin. I can walk. Really."

"Yeah, but it feels good to push on your behind. Unprofessional, but we're outside of working hours. Right?"

She giggled. "I guess so." The feel of his hands all over her was too good to complain about, anyway. He made her feel dainty.

"In fact, I'm grateful to that evil deer. Without him, I wouldn't be having this much fun."

He helped her into the truck, tucking a blanket around her legs. As promised, Joy was nestled into his jacket, completely undisturbed by the excitement her mother had just suffered. "Thank you," Kelly said. "I'm perfect now."

Nodding, he said, "You were perfect from the start."

And then he leaned in to kiss her, just a soft kiss, but it started fireworks in her heart. Kelly groaned, wishing she didn't feel her self-control slipping, but she did and she wanted more. Suddenly, the redhead inside of her took over as she turned her legs to the edge of the seat and locked them around his waist.

"Kiss me, cowboy," she said. "Kiss me like you're on fire for me."

"I think I burst into flames when I had my hand on your butt," he said before kissing her hard. "I know parts of me were definitely not feeling the wind chill."

She moaned, a sigh of pleasure, but he pulled away to look into her eyes. "Are you sure you're not hurting anywhere?"

Only my heart, she thought, and then she pulled him back to her mouth. "I want you," she said against his lips.

He stiffened with surprise, but only for a second. Then he shoved her skirt up her legs, rubbing her thighs above her knee-high boots. "Are you sure? You're okay with this?"

I'm as okay with this as any thirty-year-old red-headed, six-foot woman could ever be. She had hot, horny cowboy between her legs—he was such a strong man—she'd never be in this fantasy again in her whole life. "I know I'm not what you ordered, but—"

"Forget what I ordered. I'd say you more than meet the requirements," he said gruffly, unbuttoning her ladylike sweater. "You're too beautiful for words. You should always wear sweaters."

She giggled, slightly nervous about her size. He unsnapped her red bra from the back and then buried his face in her breasts as if he hadn't had a decent meal in weeks, and Kelly relaxed, throwing her head back, gasping as he feasted. She ran her fingers over his shoulders, burying them in his hair and knocking his hat to the ground.

"I'm sorry," she said, but he stopped her apology and awkwardness by kissing her until she was breathless. A storm rose inside her, and she squeezed her eyes shut until she felt his fingers stroking inside her thighs, creeping inside her red thong. She was slick, and that was embarrassing, so she shifted, trying to pull her legs together so he wouldn't find out. But he did. And he groaned, loud, deep, and Kelly stiffened, wondering if he was disappointed. Turned off.

But he slipped his fingers inside her, his mouth all over hers, his tongue licking inside her, and all Kelly could do was hang on to him as he pushed her to some edge she'd never been to before. Wave after wave of pleasure hit her, freezing her unexpectedly, making her cry out against his mouth.

He moved his hands to shove his jeans down, but he didn't remove his mouth from hers. In fact, he seemed to kiss her harder, as if he needed her for his very breath. She heard something like paper tearing, and Fannin muttered, "It's old, but please, let it still have staying power," and the next thing she knew, he'd moved his hands to her hips and was slowly pulling her thong down her thighs. She didn't make him do any more of the work after the thong left his hands. Moving to the very edge of the seat, she took hold of him, guiding him to her opening. He groaned again, that deep sound she loved, and then he entered her, his own passion making him thrust eagerly.

Stars of pain blinded her, but she didn't cry out. She clutched his shoulders tighter, wrapping her strong legs tightly around him, loving the feel of his passion for her. Tears came to her eyes and fell down her cheeks, but they were soaked up by the flannel of his shirt.

And then he cried out, a sound unlike anything she'd ever heard. When he slumped against her, she cradled his head to her. "Fannin?" she whispered after a moment.

"Mmm?"

"Are you all right?"

He kissed her lips tenderly. "Yeah. You?"

She was sore but happy. "Fine."

"You're pretty resilient for a woman who drove down an embankment."

She smiled into his eyes. "I come from sturdy stock."

"I'll say."

Her gaze lowered as she remembered her mother. What would she think if she saw her daughter throwing herself at a Jefferson male like this—any man, for that matter? Slowly, she reclasped her bra and buttoned her sweater while he pulled his own clothes together.

"I...can't find your, um—"

"It's okay," she said quickly, not wanting him to mention her thong. Rearranging her skirt, she pulled her knees forward into the cab.

He shut the door.

Kelly closed her eyes. Oh, Lord. Fannin was everything she'd ever wanted in a dream-come-true sexual fantasy. Of course. That's what her mother had said: the Jefferson men had that effect on women. She remembered the stories. Desperate women. All wanting exactly what she'd wanted. The brothers acted like horses' patoots, and the women chased them down anyway, so they never had to change their ways. An occasional brother got caught, but not often.

Fannin was going to be very unhappy when he discovered who she was.

And now, with her car in the ditch, she couldn't back out and go on her merry, anonymous way.

Chapter Three

"Fannin," Kelly said, her voice tight. But Fannin held up a hand, then started the truck.

"Hang on," he said.

They sat and listened. He could feel Kelly staring at him like he'd lost his mind. "I thought I heard something."

"Maybe it was my conscience ticking," she said. "Fannin, I should have told you this sooner—"

"That's what I thought." He grinned at her.

"What's what you thought?"

"Hear that sound?"

"No…"

The low, roaring sound backed up behind them. He whipped around to peer out the back window. "That would be your rescue party."

"My rescue party?"

"Yeah. While we were driving, I called my brothers to check to make certain they were taking good care of my date."

"Your date."

"Helga." He waved a hand. "It's not important. Anyway, they were already on their way back. About that time, you slid into the ditch. I mentioned they might swing through here on their way home and see if they could pull your car out." He turned to grin at her. "Of course, I thought we'd be long gone by now."

She looked a bit pale in the darkness of the truck interior. Whoops filled the background as the brothers stared down into the ditch. The sound of the two truck motors behind them was loud enough to unsettle owls. He could see why this fragile girl would be unnerved by all of it. "Don't worry. My brothers won't eat you. C'mon and meet the family."

Fannin hopped out of the truck. Kelly went out her door, coming around to the truckbed. Most of his brothers were staring down into the ditch, except for Last. And Helga, of course, probably because she was too smart to get that close to a slick edge.

"Kelly!" Helga cried out.

Kelly went flying into his housekeeper's arms. Last glanced at Fannin in surprise. Fannin shrugged, mystified. The two women embraced as if they'd known each other forever.

Finally, Kelly turned. "Fannin, this is my mother, Helga."

"My baby," Helga said.

Only Kelly was no baby. At least *he* sure didn't think so. Fannin felt his jaw sagging. "Baby?" he repeated dumbly. "Mother?"

Last turned to him. "I think that tall redhead who was in your truck said that Helga was her mother."

Fannin's heart caved. "That can't be possible. That would not be a good thing at all."

Last shook his head. "I wouldn't want those genes, either."

"No, you don't understand. I—" Fannin halted. "I mean, that would put me in a very bad spot."

"Did you know who she was? How did you meet Helga's daughter?" Last asked.

Fannin shook his head, thinking through their conversations on the phone and in person. Had Kelly ever mentioned it? He was positive he'd remember something like *Helga is my mother*.

"Dude. How are you going to fire her now?" Last asked.

"Fire who?" Fannin's thoughts were so tangled, he couldn't keep anything straight.

"Helga. Remember? We took her out tonight for the last supper, so to speak, so that you could meet your dream date—great choice, by the way, Helga's daughter and all. Makes for weird drama, doesn't it, bro?" Last slapped him on the back. "And in return for us giving up our time, you were going to speak to Mason about punting Helga over to Mimi's house."

Fannin felt ill. "I don't think I can exactly do that now."

"You have to! It was…dude, you don't understand what it was like taking Helga into Dallas. She wanted to stop and look at every point of interest, every history marker between here and there. We gave up on the movie and took her to a German restaurant instead. She had a blast, by the way.''

''I'm going to have to renege.'' He felt fairly certain that one didn't sleep with a daughter and then turn around and fire the mother. That would not be cricket. It would definitely put him in bad with Kelly, a place he did not want to be. That redhead had given him a wicked treat—and he definitely had plans for winning more of the same.

''You can't renege.'' They looked on as Kelly took her mother carefully to the side of the road to peer over, watching the brothers swarm her little car to assess the damage and develop retrieval scenarios.

''I have to. Last, I can't do it.''

''Why? You don't…you don't *like* her, do you?''

''Helga? No more than you do, but—''

''That girl.'' Last stared at him. ''You don't have the hots for Helga's daughter, do you?''

Fannin wanted to crawl under a rock to get away from Last's piercing gaze. ''She's a really nice girl.''

Last gasped. ''You realize you're putting yourself on the road to ruin, brother. Intervention may be required. You haven't thought this through.''

''Hell, I haven't thought about anything! I just now found out myself!''

''Whatever you do,'' Last said, drawing close enough so that no one could hear him, ''do not sleep with her. Understand? If you're not capable of thinking this through, then let me explain it to you in simple turns. H-e-double-hockey-sticks-ga would be your *mother-in-law*."

Fannin felt Last's sincerity blazing from his eyes.

"And if you don't know what they say about nosey, interfering mothers-in-law, you can dial up Frisco Joe and ask him what he had to do to get away from her when he was laid up with a busted leg."

"I remember," Fannin muttered.

"And mothers-in-law." Last shuddered, waving his hands for emphasis. "They are the fount of the future. You can see everything in that fount. Look closely, bro. That's what your bride would look like someday."

Fannin blinked at Last's intensity.

"And you know what they say about getting along with the in-laws and the out-laws. If you did such a thing, Fannin, that would put Helga in our family forever. Forever. She'd be ours." Last hung his head dramatically. "I could not endure it."

Fannin felt bad for his brother, even though he was a maestro of soap opera effects—until Last kicked at something on the ground.

"What's this?" Last asked, turning over a piece of red, lacy stuff on the ground with his boot.

"Nothing," Fannin said, bending to scoop Kelly's errant thong into his pocket.

"Looked like a...thong to me," Last said, his voice amazed. "Wouldn't that be strange? You see shoes all the time sitting in the middle of the road, sometimes one, sometimes two, and I always wonder who they belong to. Who so carelessly abandoned them?''

Kelly came walking back over to the truck with Helga, and Fannin growled, "Last, shut up."

"Seriously. Someone needs to do a study on how shoes get into roads, particularly at intersections in big cities. They're almost a tourist attraction in themselves. Sometimes they're hanging from telephone wires like they just got up there by themselves. I know the world is changing now that it's *undergarments* in the road...."

Kelly's eyes went wide, and Fannin was relieved that Helga didn't speak enough English to understand. "Shut *up,* Last," he reiterated, this time his voice steely.

And then Last did shut up, his eyes first on Fannin because of the tone and then sliding to Kelly's mortified expression. "Oh, brother," Last said. "Aha. I have once again allowed my philosophical side to get the best of me. If you'll excuse me, I think I'll go attach myself to the towing hitch."

He left. Fannin felt Kelly looking at him, but he couldn't look at her—not with her mother standing next to her and Kelly's red lace burning in his pocket like the world's worst-kept secret.

SLEEPING ARRANGEMENTS were easily solved once they got back to the house. Helga slept in quarters in the main house and Kelly would sleep with her mother. Only Mason remained at the big house, with Laredo, Tex and Frisco Joe having vacated the premises upon their marriages.

"You are staying awhile?" Helga asked her daughter, comfortable with chatting now that they were in her room and could speak German.

"Only one day," Kelly replied. "I don't have time off, and Julia's been out sick." She started to say that Fannin had ordered a personal assistant, and she'd chosen to fill the job since it was a Friday and wouldn't hurt for her to be gone, but as far as Helga was concerned, Kelly was here to see her.

"Oh, I miss you," her mother said.

"For Christmas, I have three days to spend with you. You're going to come to my house," Kelly promised.

"Three days?"

"Julia's sick and has been taking extra days off to get her Christmas shopping done. The office hasn't been that busy. So she said I could take three days over the holidays."

"How will I get to Diamond?"

"I'll come and get you. Don't worry, Mother. You just tell Mason you need to come home for Christmas. We're going to do lots of baking."

"Baking." Helga smiled. "It will be nice for a change to cook for someone who likes what I make."

Kelly frowned. "I know you've been homesick."

Her mother nodded. "Yes. I'm getting used to it

here. But the boys are wild.'' She gestured with her hands. ''They are too long without good women.''

Kelly winced. ''Is Fannin wild?''

Helga shrugged. ''They're all bad boys. Except Mason. He's good. Sometimes.'' She laughed.

''Sometimes?''

''I think so. He's so quiet, his heart is all bottled up inside him.''

''I love you, Mama,'' Kelly said, her insides aching for her mother. Even though Helga was speaking in a scolding tone about the brothers, Kelly could see that her mother cared about them, like rowdy chicks she wanted to keep under her wing.

Of course, that's probably not what they wanted.

''I feel bad that I sent you here, Mama, and that you're not happy. We have other ladies at the agency we could send. Why don't you come home and stay with me for a while? We'll find you another job that you'll like better. Maybe even one in Diamond?''

''I can't.'' Helga looked down at her fingers. ''The lady next door is going to have a baby. She's a real nice girl. Mimi.''

''I remember seeing Mimi's name. She's the one who called about a housekeeper.''

''Yes. She's over here all the time. I take care of her father when Mimi needs help.''

Kelly frowned. ''You're not really supposed to be doing two jobs, Mama.''

''I don't mind. I like Mimi.'' Helga sighed. ''I

think Mason is in love with Mimi. I think she's in love with him, too.''

"But she's married to someone else?" Kelly asked.

"Yes, and having a baby." Helga's eyes glowed. "A Christmas baby. I should be here to help her."

"You should be home letting me take care of you," Kelly said sternly, realizing for the first time just how much work her mother had to do at this ranch. "Mama, listen, I got a letter from Dad's estate—"

Helga held up a hand. "I don't want to talk about your father. He left me and you alone in Ireland. I made my way here. I learn English, I get some jobs, I raise my daughter. I do not want to talk about your father. He never tried to see you after we left Ireland. I do not care about him."

"Mama, he left me his house," Kelly said miserably. "I think I may go see it someday."

Helga sniffed.

"You've seen Germany, Ireland, much of Europe," Kelly said. "I've not been out of the country since I was a little girl. I want to see where my father lived. I'm sorry, Mama. I know that's hard for you. But I just need to know who I am."

"I know who you are. You are my baby," Helga said sternly.

"I know, Mama. But I need to connect with my roots." She clasped her mother's hands.

"Your roots never came to you," Helga said stubbornly. "You are like a potato. You grow your own shoots."

Kelly dropped her gaze. Her mother could have such a one-track mind. She loved her dearly, but she could definitely see how Helga and the Jefferson men might butt heads. "You go to sleep, Mama. I'm going to stay up and read for a while."

Helga got into her bed. "Thank you for surprising me with a visit. It's a long way for you to drive. Good thing Fannin came along to rescue you."

Kelly sighed. "Good night, Mama."

Joy, who Kelly had been holding, jumped up beside Grandma, recognizing where peace, comfort and warmth existed. Kelly went into the sitting room of their quarters and peered out the window. Outside, she could see men—she counted six—standing around a metal barrel with a fire blazing inside it. They were warming their hands over the fire and arguing. At least they looked as if they were arguing. She turned out the room lamp, made certain she was secured behind a drape and peered out again.

Fannin appeared to be the object of much of the conversation. Everybody was talking at him, and he just nodded or shook his head. He didn't look too happy, either. Once, she thought he glanced up at the window where she was, but then he shook his head, and she realized there was no way he could see her spying on him.

She should never have done what she did with him.

She should just get up in the morning and make a graceful exit.

Her mother wouldn't understand that at all.

One by one the brothers left the burning barrel. Only Fannin remained behind, the keeper of the flame. Kelly took a deep breath, then decided to put her conscience to rest by talking to him.

Hurrying downstairs, she slipped outside. Fannin hadn't moved from his spot. Obviously he was deep in thought.

"Fannin?"

He raised his head. "Hey, Kelly."

That didn't sound promising. She stood beside him, her heart quivering inside her. "Fannin, I owe you an apology."

He looked up. "Good. I owe you one, too."

She didn't think she could bear it if he said he was sorry for what happened between them. And yet, of course that's what he was going to say. How humiliating! The trick, then, was to make her apology and get out before she could hear those words of rejection.

If there was anything she didn't need in her life, it was for her one and only fantasy to go crashing to pieces.

"Fannin, I should have told you Helga was my mother. I should have been honest with you."

"I would have liked to have known. Everything might have turned out differently."

That was all the chance he was going to get at saying he was sorry for their interlude. "Fannin," she said briskly, "I came out here under false pretenses, so I'll leave in the morning. I'll send someone else in my place. Someone who better fits your request. We have plenty of perky, cheery blondes with great sense of humor." She'd go through every application if necessary to find him a perfect woman.

"Don't bother," he said. "I placed the order under false pretenses. I didn't really have a job for you to do. My brothers made me feel like I couldn't be successful with a woman, so I ordered a woman with all the perfect qualities of everything I wanted. And then you came along."

"Well, isn't it funny how life works out sometimes?" Kelly said brightly.

He didn't smile, and she decided this wasn't one of those made-to-order humor moments he'd wanted.

"I deceived you," he said, "and I apologize. And then I took advantage of you—"

"No, no," she said swiftly, "I took advantage of you. Clearly, I had the advantage in the advantage."

"You did not," he said. "You were a perfect lady. I practically dragged you off by the hair, just like my brothers said a woman liked."

"And did you hear me complaining? Not one bit. In fact, you may have even noticed how eager I was to shed my—" Kelly stopped, realizing she didn't want to say what she'd been about to say.

"Clothes. You didn't shed your clothes. I distinctly remember pulling them off of you." Fannin shook his head. "I am no gentleman."

"Oh, but you are," Kelly said. "Fannin, believe me, I thought you were every bit a gentleman."

"Not to take my housekeeper's daughter in my truck. I just hope the condom held. You know, I couldn't see in the darkness, but it might have been dodgy."

She frowned. "What does dodgy mean?"

"It means I couldn't examine it in the darkness. I don't know for certain that it held."

"Oh." She waved that away. "It had to. Nothing else could go wrong in this affair for me. It would be way too…corny. If you had ever told me that I would run over a dead deer, send my car into a ditch and then make love in a truck, I would have said, 'No way.'"

"I know you would have. I took advantage of the fact that you were clearly in shock."

"I was shocked," Kelly murmured, "but only that you wanted me as bad as you seemed to." The crackling blaze sucked away her words. She should have known he had been responding to goading from his brothers. "Why is there a fire in this barrel, anyway?"

"We're burning trash."

"This close to the house?"

"The hoses are closest here." Fannin didn't look up at her. "Besides, we've done this ten thousand times. We do it often, so the fire doesn't get too big."

"I see." Rural life was clearly not something one

just made up the answers to. "Hey, I'm going back inside."

For the first time, he looked at her. "Kelly, I really am sorry that I wasn't honest from the beginning."

"Neither was I."

"Yeah, but your dishonesty was a lack of information. Mine was outright deceit. You're the perfect made-to-order woman, by the way."

She stared at him. "I am?"

"Well, yeah. You're happy with darts and wine, you don't get supersqueamish about running over dead animals and you like making out in a truck. I couldn't have asked for a better date."

Her mother was right. These men were too wild for her. "Um, thanks, Fannin. Guess that's all the time we have for apologies now. Think I'll turn in so I can get up bright and early—"

His hand shot out to catch her arm. She held her breath as his gaze burned into hers. "So, when were you going to confess to being a virgin?"

Chapter Four

If there was anything Fannin was angry about—and he didn't have much to be angry about because he'd deceived her just as much as she'd deceived him—it was that Kelly obviously hadn't planned to tell him about her virginity, which she'd allowed him to take as if it didn't matter to her.

It damn sure mattered to him.

"It just wasn't in my repertoire of conversation," Kelly said. "It's not in the short list of things to say after sex, Fannin."

"I want to know why. Why did you do that? Are you husband-hunting? Did my order seem too convenient?"

"You'd be the last man I'd marry," she snapped back. "Really. Do you think my mother would approve of you?"

He frowned and let go of her arm. "So why did you do it?"

"Look. There wasn't a reason. I just wanted to. I

won't bill you, if that's what you're worried about. That would just be too weird, wouldn't it?''

Rubbing his hand over his chin, he considered the firecracker redhead in front of him. She looked mad enough to ignite a barrel fire of her own. ''Do you like me?''

''I did for about five minutes,'' she said. ''That feeling has swiftly passed.''

This was the moment where he should turn aloof and act like a Cro-Magnon man descendant. She had her reasons for what she'd done; clearly she didn't intend to reveal them to him. It bothered him, not knowing that underlying reason.

Because he really, really wanted to do the whole thing over again. Only this time, not in his truck but in a bed, where he could see every inch of that glorious body.

Too bad that wasn't going to happen.

''What are you looking at me like that for?'' she asked stiffly.

''I just can't believe you're Helga's daughter.'' What bad luck—the first woman he'd been attracted to in forever, and she was the daughter of the woman he was supposed to get off the ranch!

''Well, I am. Now you know.''

Mason pulled up in his truck, reminding Fannin of the unpleasant conversation he had to have with his brother. A matter which wouldn't endear him to Kelly, that was for certain.

''Mason, can I talk to you a minute?''

Mason slammed his truck door and ambled over. "Hi," he said to Kelly.

"This is Kelly Stone, Helga's daughter," Fannin said.

"Helga's daughter. Well, welcome to the ranch! I didn't know you were coming out." Mason beamed. "Helga's really worked out for us."

Kelly gave Fannin a very wry glance. Fannin shrugged.

"Are you here for the holidays?" Mason asked. "We'd love for you to stay."

"She's here for a short visit," Fannin said quickly. "Kelly's got a very busy schedule."

Kelly blinked at Fannin's tone. He couldn't have said any more plainly how he felt about her presence at the ranch.

"Well, that's a shame. With Christmas being next weekend, things are really going to be hopping around here. And I'm sure your mother would love to have her daughter here with her. Everybody wants their loved ones around at Christmas."

Kelly saw Mason's gaze flicker, ever so quickly, to the house on the adjoining land. Mimi's house. Kelly's heart turned over inside her. "Well, I'm going to turn in," she said. "Good night, Fannin. It's nice to meet you, Mason."

Mason tipped his hat to her. "Pleasure's mine."

Kelly walked away, making it inside the doors and toward the stairwell before Fannin's voice stopped her.

"It's about Helga, Mason. They've asked me to talk to you about her."

The window was open in the kitchen, cracked to let cool air in and probably to let the cooking smells out. Helga had always said she didn't like to smell food after it had been cooked and eaten. Kelly crept close to the window.

"They don't want Helga to be the housekeeper anymore."

"Tough. They don't live here. I do. And as far as I can remember, they come here every night to eat in the main kitchen with barely a word of complaint."

"They do complain, just not in your hearing. Look, Mason, the truth is, we've all been tiptoeing around this for a year. Helga isn't the one who put the curtains up, she's not the one who held everything together during the big storm. The Lonely Hearts ladies did all that." Fannin took a deep breath. "Mason, you're not going to want to get this wake-up call, but Mimi hired Helga to keep you from hiring a housekeeper you might fall for."

"What's that supposed to mean?"

Kelly shivered, realizing she was eavesdropping on a highly personal disagreement. She excused herself by thinking the best thing she could do was to protect her mother—and to do that, she needed to know the score.

"What are you talking about, Fannin?" Mason asked.

"The first woman to come in this house was An-

nabelle and her baby, Emmie. Mimi panicked, realizing that a sweet young housekeeper with a ready-
made family might be all it took for her to lose you
forever. So she hired Helga. To keep you, you know,
fed and taken care of. So you wouldn't feel lonely.
And you know what, Mason? It's worked.''

''Nonsense.''

''Have you had any real dates? Have you gone out
with anyone? What do you do all day? Moon after
Mimi, who's gone on with her life, if you haven't
noticed. And eat Helga's cooking.''

''And your solution to this is?''

''Let's send Helga over to Mimi's, where she be-
longs. Mimi needs her. We don't. The boys want to
be alone.''

''We need a housekeeper.''

''No, Mason,'' Fannin said quietly. ''You need to
put the past behind you and move on. We're all a
year older since the big storm and the e-mail that
brought the Lonely Hearts ladies out here. Four of the
brothers are gone. They were the lucky ones. They
found ladies they loved. The rest of us, we're just
sinking in quicksand.''

Kelly gasped. ''Butt-head!''

Fannin glanced up. ''Did you hear something?''

Mason shook his head. ''No. Just your opinions
wearing me out. I'm tired. Can we do this later over
a family council or something?''

''I guess. Thing is, Mason, you're not the only one
with needs around here. 'Night.''

"Hey," Mason said. "How'd Kelly end up here, anyway? I don't remember Helga mentioning she was going to have a visitor."

Kelly strained to hear Fannin's answer.

"Long story, bro. Not that interesting. See ya in la mañana."

"I'll give him *not that interesting*." Kelly scrambled to her feet and shot up the stairs to her mother's quarters before Mason could catch her spying.

Fannin was such a traitor! She couldn't believe she'd ever thought he was a gentleman. Good thing she knew now exactly how he felt about women, about her mother—even about her. First thing in the morning, she was going to talk to her mother about leaving this horrible place.

Obviously, it was no place for a lady.

In the morning, everyone gathered at the breakfast table to eat.

Sauerkraut and sausages.

"Mmm, my favorite," Mason said. He tucked in heartily, much to Fannin's annoyance.

To his greater annoyance, Kelly looked like sunshine. She wore a canary-yellow, long-sleeved dress that made her hair shine. Her blue eyes never met his gaze, though, and that bothered him.

She was playing aloof, probably.

He resolved to be more aloof, too. Like his brothers, who were currently staring at their plates in dismay.

Kelly, on the other hand, had his total concentration.

He wanted her in a bed. Bad.

Last night's conversation with Mason would mean Helga would leave, at least their house. He might not ever see Kelly again after this week.

Taking an absent-minded bite of sausage, he wondered if she was wearing a thong today. The red lacy thing Last had discovered on the ground was now tucked away in Fannin's closet, a secreted jewel he was hoarding.

He should return it, but why? Wasn't he old enough to develop a panty fixation? Probably past time, anyway. Every one of the brothers had their sin. He was keeping Kelly's thong for the memories, if nothing else. His only virgin.

Frowning, he chewed at something he'd picked up off his plate. Scalps were prizes in olden days. Ladies were reputed to keep lists of men they conquered. Men supposedly notched their bedposts. He wondered if keeping a thong ranked as a trophy.

Last cleared his throat and shoved his arm. "You're eating your napkin, bro," he said.

Fannin spat what he was chewing onto his plate. Damn if Kelly hadn't laid a napkin near his plate, with one edge flapping over his breakfast. He'd scooped it up with some sauerkraut and chewed away, most of the napkin hanging from his jowls.

Kelly was staring at him, her hand arrested over the stove. His brothers were grinning.

Except Mason, who looked thunderous.

"Ch, ch." Helga gave him the naughty-boy sound and retrieved his napkin, taking it into the laundry. She came over and tied a fresh one around his neck. "Do not eat," she said in her thick German-accented voice as she pointed at the napkin under his chin.

Kelly merely returned to washing dishes in the sink.

"You need table manners," Mason told him sternly.

"That's *it*." Fannin tore the napkin off his neck, tossed it on the table and left. Being babied by Helga was too much. He had his mind on her daughter, and she was treating him like a child in front of Kelly.

Kelly appeared at his elbow, trotting to keep up. "Fannin, my mother means well."

"I know." But he kept walking.

She stopped him by putting a hand on his arm. He didn't look at her, too irritated and uncomfortable to make eye contact.

"Fannin, maybe we should start over."

He glared at her. "Like, you're going to grow a new hymen and this time tell me you're a virgin?"

"Like, maybe you're going to be honest about wanting a woman and not a personal-assistant-slash-companion?" She returned his glare.

"What exactly did you have in mind, then, as we start over?"

"Let's tell each other the truth from now on."

"That would be novel."

She put her hands on her hips. "Listen, buster, I can be just as sarcastic as you." Pointing to her hair, she said, "Hair this color has a reputation for a reason. How about you give me a chance before my temper sets on fire?"

He sighed. "Shoot."

"All right. I heard you talking to Mason about letting my mother go."

"Okay, that's embarrassing, but…what can I tell you. It happened. I'm sorry. It's the way my brothers feel." He was sorry for the pain that crossed her sweet face, but she wanted honesty.

"You don't like her, either, do you?"

"Kelly, I try. But it's hard when she treats us like children."

She looked at the ground. "You're right."

He felt bad, but the situation wasn't pretty. "Kelly, I wish I'd known who you were. I wouldn't have touched you."

"Thanks, Fannin, you ass. That just makes me feel so much better. You don't like my mother and you wish you'd never had sex with me."

"That's not what I said. I've thought of what happened between us a lot. That was more than what I thought I was going to get when I e-mailed the Honey-Do Agency, believe me." He softened his tone. "But, Kelly, I wouldn't have touched you if you'd told me who you were, and you knew it. Or you would have been up-front with me.''

''You're right.'' She lowered her gaze for just an instant, then looked back at him. ''I'm sorry, Fannin, not only for not being truthful but also for my mother. As part of the Honey-Do Agency, I need to be professional here.''

''Okay.'' He wondered where she was going with that.

''I can offer you two options, now that I'm aware you're unhappy with your employee. I can talk to Mama and let her know she needs to try not to make you all her children. And whatever other changes you'd like her to make. You'd have to tell me exactly what needs to happen, because she's my mother and I think she's an angel. Stubborn, but an angel.''

He felt really bad about that. The brothers all felt that their mother had been an angel, too. Frowning, he wondered if Last wasn't the only member of the family who saw life through the rose-colored glasses Mason always teased him about.

''Or I can talk to Mama and Mimi about Mama going to work next door. Your choice. Whichever option you think would work best for your situation.''

He admired the hell out of her for taking the bull by the horns. ''It might be best if you referenced Mason on that one. I've done my part, which was to be the bearer of bad news. And since I'm the one who has defiled the daughter and dumped on the mother, I'd say my work here is done. Or it better be.''

''Okay. I'll talk to Mason.''

She turned and walked away. He watched her, canary yellow moving at a fast pace, swing, bang, boom. She was a big lady, with hips he wanted to sink his teeth into. And other things, too. When they'd been having their honest chat, she'd met him eye to eye, boot toe to boot toe.

He liked that. It made him think of all kinds of rowdy sexual positions he could get into with a woman built for him.

Too bad it was all so damn wrong. His order might have been placed and it might have been filled, but it was wrong on every level.

He stared out at Princess, who was at the other end of the pasture from Bloodthirsty Black. ''Yeah,'' he said to his brown-eyed pet, ''I know what it means to have the right thing under your nose, and not be able to do a damn thing with it.''

KELLY WALKED AWAY, her heart pounding. Whatever might have been possible between Fannin and her was never going to happen now. If it hadn't been bad enough that Helga was her mother—and she had to give Fannin credit that he'd tried to be kind to Helga, but what man wanted a napkin tied around his neck?—Kelly hadn't been honest from the start.

Fannin was right, and she knew it.

Professionalism was her only alternative at this point. Cool, calm professionalism.

The first thing she had to do was talk to Mason. And then her mother, who wasn't going to understand. She was only being a good mother; overnurturing was what Helga knew from the old world. Still Kelly understood that the brothers wouldn't be comfortable with that.

She turned to sneak a glance at Fannin as she stepped up on the porch—and was startled to see the cowboy staring back at her. Even across a half acre of land, she knew he was watching her.

It made her nervous. Clearly, he didn't like her.

Professionalism, she reminded herself—and then a swift exit.

"Hey," Archer said as he walked out onto the porch. "Kelly, lend me your keys."

"What for?"

"I'm gonna go hose the deer guts off your car."

"Eeew. That's a job I'll let you do. Thanks."

"I have to. Your mother's already out there with a bucket. That woman can spot dirt a mile away."

"Mama!" Kelly gasped. "Where is she?"

"We parked your car around back. Where's your keys?"

"Bandera had them last!" Kelly took off at a run. Sure enough, Helga was busy with a towel, a sponge and a large bucket of water that steamed in the early-morning chill. "Mama, no! Stop!"

Helga straightened. "Why?"

"Because." Kelly blushed. When she'd told her mother about the run-in with the deer last night, she hadn't thought her mother would try to clean it up! The brothers had towed the car home, and she'd been too happy to ride to the ranch with Fannin. "It's not necessary, Mama," she said in German. "Archer's going to take the truck to the car wash."

"I'll clean it." Helga frowned and went back to scrubbing.

Of course she would think it was wasteful to take the car to a car wash when she could do the job herself. Kelly looked at her mother's set face and her red, chapped hands and wanted to cry.

Before she realized what was happening, Fannin strode to her mother and gently removed the sponge from her fingers. He tossed it into the bucket, which he then emptied. "Go upstairs and change," he told Helga. "Get Joy, and the three of you go shopping. Day off."

"No. Not day off," Helga said.

"It is now," Fannin said with quiet determination. "Spend a day with your daughter, Helga. You deserve it."

Kelly flashed him a grateful glance. "Yes, Mama. Come on. You deserve a holiday."

"Christmas is next week," Helga stated.

"Yes, but—" Kelly glanced around, her eyes lighting on a heavily pregnant woman walking across the field toward the Jefferson house. That had to be Mimi, who she'd heard about from Julia. "But we need to go baby shopping, right, Mama? First Christmas for the baby."

Helga saw Mimi and brightened instantly. "Yes." She turned and walked into the house.

Kelly closed her eyes briefly with relief. When she opened them, Archer was getting into the car and Fannin was hosing out the bucket. Everything was going on as normal. There was just a little extra work for them to do because of Kelly and her mother...work that didn't need to be added to her load at the ranch.

Fannin didn't look her way.

Kelly's heart constricted. *So be it,* she thought. *I completely understand.* "Thank you," she said. "Mama will enjoy a day off."

He grunted and tears came to Kelly's eyes. They needed help—but they weren't getting it. It was all wrong.

She went to find her mother.

MIMI WATCHED FANNIN put away a bucket, sponge and hose. "Isn't it cold to be washing a car?"

"Maybe. How are you doing, Mimi? Feeling good?"

She put a hand over her very large stomach. "I'm not supposed to be walking much, but I'm going stir-crazy. I wish I could get out. I'd like to ride. I'd like to do anything."

"It's not much longer," he said, comforting her.

"I know. And I'm glad about the baby. You know that. It's just inactivity has never been my thing."

He grinned at her. "I know. How's the sheriff?"

"Having one of his good days. That's why I decided to get out and see the outdoors for a minute."

Of course, what she really wanted was to see Mason, God help her. She was nervous as could be, more nervous than she'd ever been in her life. Her husband Brian was in Houston, working a big legislative case. He had to be gone; she understood that. Brian had said he'd be back in time for Christmas, in time for the baby's birth. Nothing would keep him from her side, he'd said.

Mimi knew Brian meant it.

Still, she was nervous. "Where's Mason?"

Fannin looked at her strangely. Was it pity she saw in his eyes?

She held her ground, staring right back. As if she had every right to ask where Mason was. There'd been a subtle shift in the Jefferson men's behavior toward her, ever since she'd become pregnant. Almost as if they felt she shouldn't hang around Mason. But they'd always been friends and they always would be.

"Mason's…inside," Fannin said after a moment.

"Thanks." Mimi hated feeling as if she didn't belong to the clan anymore. She knew they still loved her, but there was a strange distance in the air that had never been there before.

"You know, Mimi—"

Mimi whirled to stare Fannin down. If he said a word about her wanting to see Mason, she was going to grab that hose and give him a washdown he'd *never* forget. It's really best if he doesn't mess with a big, fat, nervous pregnant woman. "Yes?"

Fannin sighed. "Nothing."

"Are you sure?" she snapped.

"Positive. Lasso those hormones, sister. I need my head a few more days, anyway."

Mimi gave him a black look and stomped away.

Chapter Five

Fannin watched as Mimi left, then he turned to put the hose away. Fiery women, Mimi and Kelly. "Wish I'd seen that coming," he muttered.

"Seen what coming?" Kelly asked, walking past him to her car.

"You, for starters. Do you always sneak up on people?"

"Only people who are standing right next to my car." She opened the passenger side door, helping her mother in. "Is Mimi having a boy or a girl?"

"How would I know?" Fannin demanded.

"Because you live next door, and she might have told you," Kelly said reasonably. "Mama doesn't know about the sex, either."

"What?" Fannin looked guiltily at the German housekeeper, but she was settling Joy into her lap.

Kelly looked at him curiously. "Mama doesn't know the sex of Mimi's baby."

He stared at her.

"Oh," Kelly said with a frown, "you weren't thinking I told my mom about us—"

"No!" He didn't want to talk about sex, not with her mother between them, even if Helga didn't understand what they were saying. His skin felt like it was hiving. "Don't even mention it."

"I didn't. You did." She got into the car and rolled the window down to talk across her mother. "Thanks for washing off my car."

"It's fine."

He earned a frown from her for that answer. She rolled the window back up. He walked around to her side of the car and tapped on the window.

She rolled it down.

"Where are you going?" he asked.

"Shopping."

"I know. Where?"

She glared at him. "Does it matter? In the grand scheme of life?"

"Not really."

"Well, then I don't need to give you an itinerary, do I?"

He sighed, scratching his head under his hat. "Will you call if you get lost?"

"Thank you, but I think I can find my way around a small town."

"Oh." She wasn't going far, another relief, although he couldn't say why. "Can I talk to you when you get back?"

"Topic?"

"I'm not really ready to discuss it. I need to formulate my thoughts."

She frowned. "That sounds serious."

He glanced at Helga. "I'm sorry about everything."

"I am, too. If you are, then I most definitely am."

He nodded.

"I'll leave after I take Mama shopping."

"I understand."

"By the way, have you decided about what you want me to tell her?"

"We're trying to make a family decision about that. As of now, no. Let's just leave it through Christmas." It would be unfair to make any changes before the holidays.

"Mimi looks awfully big. When is she due?"

"Anyday now, I think." He stared down at Kelly, wondering how eyes like hers could be so blue. How could red hair be that crisp and vibrant? It looked so soft and yet the color was so shiny. You wouldn't miss this woman—she was simply dynamite. "Have a good time," he said.

"Goodbye," was her reply as she rolled up the window.

But she stared at him a second longer than it took for the window to roll up—and in her gaze he saw sadness.

He'd put that sadness there.

Sighing, he tapped on the window again. She rolled her eyes, but she obliged him.

"Kelly, under the circumstances I probably shouldn't say this, but…you…I mean, I can go with you, if you'd like. Chauffeur the two of you. Carry packages. Joy," he said, his words rambling so that he wouldn't say what he really wanted to say, that she looked deliciously pretty. He thought about the hidden thong, and his face felt very flushed.

"It won't solve anything."

He sighed. "I don't want to solve anything. I'm trying to establish a set of good manners where you're concerned."

Slowly she opened the door and stood to meet him, face-to-face, the way he liked. He was glad his request for petite had gone unfilled.

"I'll ride in the back seat," she said. "You need to get to know Mama better."

This was a battle he wasn't going to win, he could tell. He wasn't even going to reach for a weapon—she'd gun him down. Kelly was going for safety. With Mama squarely up front, Kelly was protected from further advances from him.

Which just flipped on his Determined switch.

This lady didn't know it yet, but she hadn't seen the last of his romancing.

"THERE THEY GO," Last said as he watched Kelly's car pull down the drive with Fannin at the wheel. "A jackass, a redhead, a minidog and a housekeeper from hell. Where's *Sorriest Home Videos* when you need it?"

"Fannin sure is making a project out of Helga," Archer said. He sat at the kitchen table, not doing much, along with Calhoun and Navarro, while Last spied.

Navarro shrugged. "At least he's not festering over Princess. Maybe he'll give up on her and do it the easy way. No muss, no fuss."

"That's the problem," Last said. "We have too much muss and fuss around here."

Archer glanced up from reading the funny papers. "Specifically?"

"I think Fannin's sweet on Helga's daughter."

He now had his brothers' full attention.

"Sweet? She's only been here one night," Calhoun said.

"Enough time to do significant damage to a man who likes to do everything the hard way," Last stated.

Archer's eyes bugged. "Are you going somewhere with this?"

Last sighed. "Remember when we discussed the Quest for Truth, finding out what really happened to Dad when he left after Mom died?"

The brothers nodded, their gazes sliding away.

"And Fannin said he'd head up the inquiry? Remember?"

"Yes!" Archer glared. "We remember. Move on, okay?"

"I'm just saying I don't think a lot of looking's going to be going on now that he's got *her*."

"Got her?" Calhoun shook his head. "He wouldn't get Kelly. Bank on that."

Navarro nodded. "Second that."

Last sighed at their innocence. "Pay attention, numbskulls. Fannin likes her. And that could mean all our plans go up in smoke. Picture it, all our planning to get Helga moved over to Mimi—moot. Because she becomes our mother-in-law."

Archer laughed. "Not gonna happen, dude."

"It's happened."

Calhoun looked at him. "What happened, philosopher?"

"*It* happened."

There was silence around the table as his brothers digested the syllabic emphasis.

"Nah," Archer said. "Not Fannin. He's a slow mover. A creepy-crawler. A tortoise. Not the kind to sneak around the house where a mother is sleeping, for heaven's sake."

His brothers went back to what they were doing, which was not a damn thing as far as Last was concerned. He needed action and he needed it five minutes ago.

Last felt desperate. "You guys don't want to listen now, but I know things you don't. And you're not going to be happy."

"You've always known things we didn't, little bro," Calhoun said mildly. "We overlook you when you get too hopped up on yourself."

"It's going to interfere with the Quest for Truth,"

Last pointed out. "Fannin's got his mind on Kelly. He's not even paying attention to Princess!"

"That's a good thing," Archer said. "I always say, too long without a woman and that man might've started looking funny at his livestock."

The brothers snickered to themselves.

"We need to make sure this ends now, before it ever gets started," Last stated. "More than it already has."

The comics section got tossed onto the table. "Exactly what do you want from us, Last?" Archer asked.

"We need to continue with the plan to move Helga, first off. Secondly, we need to make sure her daughter leaves here pronto."

"If Mason knows you're plotting against him, your head's gonna roll," Navarro pointed out.

"Yeah, and if Helga becomes Fannin's mother-in-law, your dinner's gonna roll, every day for the rest of your lives!" Last didn't see any point in reminding them that the situation was dire—the rooster had already been in the chicken coop, and heaven help all of them if an egg had been laid. "Look," he said, "I'll keep Fannin busy. Y'all get rid of Kiss-Me Kelly and her little red dog, too."

"You sound like the witch in *The Wizard of Oz.* And your little dog, too," Calhoun mimicked.

"Whatever," Last said. "You'll enjoy your positions as best men at the wedding, I'm sure."

"But what if he likes her? Isn't that his business?" Navarro asked. "Should we be playing the heavies?

Maybe we should let matters run their course so Fannin won't be p'od with us.''

Last thought about the thong on the ground. ''What I think is that Kelly's probably heard from her mother how nice we all are and how wonderful ranch life is. And she set out to get herself a Jefferson male.''

''Well, she wouldn't be the first,'' Archer said.

''And probably not the last,'' Last said. ''I think we just better make sure poor Fannin doesn't get taken. He's already been taken in,'' Last said, not appreciating his own irony. ''I mean, by a wily female.''

''All right,'' Navarro said. ''We're in. All for one and one for all.''

''Save a Jefferson male and you save a good man from extinction,'' Calhoun agreed.

Archer folded up the funny papers. ''A free range male is healthy, happy and primo.''

Last grinned weakly from relief. ''Once again, we save the family ranch from dishonorable intentions.''

''But say, just say,'' Archer said, ''that Kelly's intentions are honorable.''

The red thong came to mind one last time. No nice girl met a man for the first time and lost her thong. ''Trust me on this,'' Last said. ''I know dishonorable intentions when I see them. Intervention is *required*.''

''MAMA'S SO HAPPY picking out things for the baby,'' Kelly said to Fannin as they strolled along the square in town. ''Thank you for bringing her.''

Fannin walked beside her, big and strong in the crisp December air, holding Joy inside his jacket. He claimed Joy preferred body warmth to the Coach bag she generally rode in, but Kelly thought Fannin had a possible soft spot he didn't want anyone to see.

"I didn't have anything else to do."

Kelly smiled. Fannin had plenty to do, but for some reason he'd decided to accompany them. Which she thought was sweet. They watched as Helga picked up baby booties, a hat and some pretty blankets. "Wonder why Mama dislikes you so much."

"Me? She dislikes me?"

She smiled at him. "Well, all of you. She says you're wild men."

"I am not wild."

Fannin eyed her lips, making Kelly automatically swipe her tongue along her mouth. It was a primal reaction, but she couldn't help it.

"Are your brothers?"

He grinned. "Yeah."

"Proud of that, are you?"

"Not proud, necessarily, just laughing with them."

She didn't like that. A good man would see the difference between wild and fun. One was worth keeping, the other was not. "Laughter is like applause."

"Did I laugh when you rolled down the ditch?"

"No." She wondered where he was going with that.

"Well, I am now, since I know you're not hurt and

everything's fine.'' He shrugged. "That's how I feel about my brothers. We're vastly different. But I applaud their actions when they're amusing.''

Helga came over to them, scowling up at Fannin, clearly allowing her feelings to show. Then she held out her selections for Kelly to examine before walking away again.

"I don't know,'' Kelly murmured. "Mama doesn't seem that sold on you. Maybe you're not being totally candid with me.''

"And you might be looking for someone who wouldn't ask too many questions.''

She sent him a disbelieving look. "About what?''

He shrugged and glanced away. "Oh, like, what's a nice girl like you doing in my truck with your panties off, kind of stuff. The truth is,'' he said, getting close, "I think you were looking for a wild man so that you could let go of some of the goody two-shoes you've built into your world. I think you came out here to find a man to make you feel like you'd lived life. Instead of being cloistered in your mother's mold.''

She blinked.

"I'm right, aren't I?'' Joy shifted inside his jacket, and Fannin glanced down for just a moment. When he looked back up, his eyes were dark and penetrating. "Are you longing to visit someplace new? Maybe a foreign country? You're thirty, right? Your mother's out here with us, and you're working the same job, day in, day out. You're probably starting to question what you've done with your life. It's pretty normal, actually, to reassess at that age. Textbook case. You're looking for a husband.''

A gasp escaped her.

He held up a hand. ''You want a fling, so you can find the right man for you. Then when the dishes pile up and the kids never pick up their clothes, you can look back and say to yourself, 'I lived. I had this one really wild night in a truck with a cowboy and I lost my virgin—'''

''That's enough!'' She forced a smile for her mother and took the things she was holding over to the register. ''You're awful, you know it?''

Fannin laughed. ''I'm honest.''

KELLY AND FANNIN ATE dinner with her mother that night, then took her home. Neither of them was willing to claim victory after the wild-man conversation, but Fannin felt he had Kelly on the run. If she'd ever thought he was some uninteresting, pliable, run-me-over-and-don't-look-back kind of guy, he'd certainly turned her thoughts around.

He didn't want her thinking too much. There was far too much going on between them for him to lose her right away. His brothers' method of keeping women interested was just the potion—so far it seemed to be working.

She stared at him over the mashed potatoes in the center of the table. He stared right back. His brothers were all grouped around the table, and he and Kelly had been placed as far away from each other as they could possibly get. Whoever was in charge of the placards was going to be shot at sunrise, he vowed— he wanted her close to him.

Calhoun and Mason were sitting on either side of Kelly, and Calhoun appeared to enjoy the seating chart. Fannin scowled as Calhoun handed the bowl of broccoli to Kelly and forked some broccoli onto her plate. As if he were a gentleman. Which he wasn't, and Kelly would be too smart to fall for that worn-out gag.

But maybe she wasn't. She had been a virgin. Not that being a virgin made her dumb, but she hadn't been exposed to the animal magnetism his brothers were reputed to possess. And she was *his* virgin, damn it.

Fannin steamed inside his flannel shirt.

Mason, as usual, appeared to be immune to anything except the food on his plate. "Mason, could you pass the broccoli?" Fannin asked in a bid to get Kelly's eyes on him.

"Wait your turn," Mason said sourly. "We always go counterclockwise with the bowls."

And who made up that stupid rule, Fannin thought. Kelly looked at him, just a quick glance, then looked away. All right, so she wasn't quite as hooked as he wanted her to be.

Time to pour on some more of his brothers' catch-me-if-you-can charm. "I'm going out," he said abruptly, standing and tossing his napkin to the table.

Now Kelly's eyes were on him.

"Where are you going?" Archer asked.

"Out," Fannin replied curtly.

"You're being rude as hell to our guest," Mason said.

"Beg your pardon, ma'am," he said, and then left the room.

But not before he saw the grin on Last's face.

"You'll have to excuse him," Fannin heard Last say. "He can be moody."

"Yes," Navarro said, "very sideways about his broccoli. By the way, your mother is a wonderful cook."

Fannin hovered in the hall, eavesdropping shamelessly.

"Really?" Kelly asked. "Do you think so?"

Her voice held doubt and suspicion. Fannin was suspicious, too. There was a reason his brothers were being so nice to Helga's daughter—nothing good could come of its ploy.

They always had a tactic to play, an ace they were hiding.

"I'm outta here," he said to himself. "Absence makes the heart grow fonder."

But then the front door blew open, very nearly cold-cocking him, and Mimi stumbled into his arms.

"I feel strange," she said, moaning.

Chapter Six

Fannin struggled to hold Mimi up.

"Mimi feels strange!" he hollered, not knowing what else to say. Mimi's entire weight was against him, and he knew her well enough to know that she wouldn't be dead weight in his arms if she could help it.

Mason came running, practically leaping over chairs to get to Mimi. "Hold on, Mimi. Lay her on the sofa. Last, call Doc Gonzalez. Helga—"

But he didn't have to instruct Helga, because Helga was already fussing over Mimi, making certain her feet were up and sweeping her hair away from her brow. Kelly crouched beside her mother, and the two of them burst into rapid German.

Fannin stood helplessly, out of his league.

"Don't just stand there! Do something!" Mason exclaimed. "Everybody get towels. Boil water!"

"Calm down, bro." Fannin went to stand beside his brother. "She's going to be fine."

"She doesn't look fine," Mason said, his face drawn. "She looks freaking ill."

Mimi did not look good. Since she wasn't the type to play the wan, fainting heroine, Fannin knew as well as Mason did that something wasn't right.

"Where's the damn doctor?" Mason growled.

"On his way," Last said. "Take a deep breath, Mason. Don't pop a coronary on us."

"I'm gonna pop you—"

"Shh!" Kelly looked up at the brothers, who were clustered around the sofa. "Go out and burn a fire in a barrel or something, okay? Mimi needs quiet. Not a bunch of overreacting males hanging around her, losing their nerve."

Every man in the room stared at her.

Helga glanced up, her gaze warning.

"My mother requests that you find someplace else to light. We'll call you when we need help," Kelly said more gently.

Silently the men filed out. They perched on porch rails and stared out at the dark fields or sat heavily on the porch step. Mason stood where he could see through the window. He wasn't obvious about it, but Fannin knew what he was doing.

"Damn Doc Gonzalez anyway," Mason said. "A man that old oughta retire. He drives so slow that—"

"Mason. Cool it," Fannin demanded. "She's not pregnant with your child, okay? Somebody figure out how to put a call into Brian."

Mason stopped bitching. He remained there, his hands in his pockets, looking helpless.

Fannin frowned. "I'm sorry, Mason."

"It's fine. You're right."

Then his brother turned his back to him and the drama going on inside the house. Fannin sighed. "I'll go call Brian." He could find the number if he tried hard enough. And he figured someone needed to check on the sheriff. Going back inside, he noted Helga had Mimi quiet now, a cloth on her forehead. Mimi seemed much calmer. Kelly glanced up at him as she sat beside her mother, and he felt the stir inside him he was beginning to associate with her.

Little bit bad girl, she was. But ever so cautious.

"Mimi, I'm going to call Brian," he said, ignoring Helga's glare.

"No." Mimi opened her eyes. "Do not call my husband."

He glanced at Kelly. "Mimi—"

"I don't want Brian to know I'm not feeling well. It's going to pass in a moment. Helga says I just got nervous. Don't bother Brian over something trivial."

Kelly watched him curiously.

"Are you sure you don't want me to call Brian? It's no trouble."

"Fannin," Kelly said, "she says not to. Brian's got a big court case he's working right now, and she doesn't want him bothered. Mama says Mimi's going to be fine. Now go back out and tell everybody to *relax*."

He'd be the last one to know about women, pregnant women especially. Kelly seemed to think the situation was under control. Not wanting to seem out of his depth, which he was, he backed out of the room and closed the door.

"Think they've got it under control," he told Mason. "Think we're supposed to go count grass blades in the yard or something."

"It's December, dummy," Mason said crossly. "How much grass do you see?"

"Don't jump on me, Mason. I'm doing the best I can with three ornery females and you eating my head!" He glared at Mason for emphasis.

"Here comes Doc Gonzalez, at the best moment," Last said. "Before this whole place blows up over a *baby*. Interesting how much havoc a pregnant woman can wreak on men's perfectly normal existences, isn't it?"

But no one was in the mood for Last and his deep ponderings.

"Hey, Doc," Fannin called. "Thanks for coming out. Mimi wouldn't let us take her into Dallas."

"It's fine, boys. Been a while since I've been out, hasn't it?" He peered at them as he stamped his feet clean on the doormat. "Since Frisco Joe broke his leg last year, maybe? Or was it Laredo's concussion? Or Ranger's—"

"Doc, Mimi's in here," Fannin said hurriedly, before the Curse of the Broken Body Parts—a fairy tale of Laredo's if he'd ever heard one—could be visited

on him. Who really thought the Jefferson brothers had
to be injured before they fell in love? After all, Mason
was suffering from a different curse—Broken Heart
Syndrome, if Fannin was any judge.

Of course, as of yesterday, Fannin was determined
not to end up like his brothers, the jugheads. They'd
avoided love. He was going to find meaningful sex
with the redhead inside—if it killed him. She was his
made-to-order girl, even if the wrong order had arrived.

He wasn't looking a gift horse in the mouth.
"Kelly, can I see you?" he said, as Doc Gonzalez
went inside.

"Not now, Fannin." Kelly shook her head at him.
"I'm not leaving Mama."

"She's fine. The doctor's here."

"I'm not leaving my mother, Fannin. She doesn't
understand much English, as hard as she tries. I don't
think she's in the best environment for learning it."

Kelly looked away, listening to what Doc Gonzalez
was murmuring to Mimi. Fannin stood thunderstruck.
Had Kelly just accused their family of mistreating her
mother? He had certainly tried to be accommodating,
more so than his brothers. He squinted at the redhead,
who was intent on the matter at hand. Sighing, he
went off to a corner to wait until they determined if
an ambulance, a hot meal or an absent husband was
needed for Mimi. Whatever it was, he was determined
to be of service.

Anything to get close to Kelly.

KELLY TRIED TO IGNORE the big cowboy propped in the corner, but it was hard. For one thing, he was snoring slightly, asleep the moment he'd hit the chair. She reminded herself that they'd been up late the night before, and no doubt he found their current dilemma painstakingly slow. He was a man of action and it seemed that, for now, they were in a holding pattern.

"I'm sending you home, Mimi," Doc Gonzalez said. "You need to be in bed until this baby comes. Mostly, you need help. I want you to put a call in to your regular physician and tell him that you're worn out."

"It's a her," Mimi said tiredly. "I went to the doctor who presided at the rodeo, the one all the Jefferson boys thought was so pretty. She's very smart, and she agreed to help me find a midwife so I could have the baby at home."

"What?" Mason had come in to hear what Doc had to say, and his whole body went rigid. "You can't do that, Mimi! It's dumb!"

She'd been pale, Kelly noticed, until Mason's pig-headed statement. And then it seemed life was breathed into Mimi through stubborn, determined, prideful will. "It's not dumb, Mason. You just shut *up*."

Everyone was silent for a moment.

Then Fannin said, "Well, just like old times around here now, isn't it?" which broke the ice and made everyone laugh, except Kelly, who wondered if it re-

ally was like old times or if everybody was just doing
an amazing job of hiding their true feelings.

"I'll go over and stay with Mimi," she said suddenly.

"No," Helga said, "I go with Mimi." And she
patted Mimi's hand telling Kelly what she planned to
do.

"Mama has decided to move over to Mimi's,"
Kelly told Fannin. "She says the sheriff and Mimi
need her." There, she thought, that ought to make
everybody happy.

And for some reason that made her mad—at Fannin. She couldn't help remembering the conversation
she'd overheard. And the order he'd e-mailed in to
the Honey-Do Agency, as if he expected the world to
be so easy for him that he could ask for the perfect
woman. He'd tried to camouflage it as a work request,
but she knew better.

He'd been shopping. The man did like to shop. She
knew that firsthand from their stroll in town, where
the ladies had hung out from shop doors to call hello.
She'd seen one girl give him a hug that was far from
just-bein'-friendly.

She knew just what Mr. Hard Case needed.

"I'm going to stay here, Mason," she announced.

"Oh, sure, of course. Whatever you need."

"Oh, no. It's a matter of what *you* need," she said
sweetly, her gaze deliberately on Fannin. "You'll
need housekeeping help. Mama needs me close by.

And the Honey-Do Agency must keep their clients happy. This is a wonderful solution for everyone.''

Fannin stared at her.

"Now, you don't need to do housekeeping here," Mason said uncomfortably. "You're a guest at our ranch."

"I'd rather earn my keep, if you don't mind. I'll take Mama's job, and she can do what she feels called to do." She smiled at Fannin. "I know how happy that will make everyone."

She didn't miss the concerned glances the men threw each other. Boy, she had a surprise for them. They were going to wish they'd been nice to her mother—especially Mr. Cocky.

And she went upstairs to unpack.

The brothers watched as Fannin headed up the stairs, purpose in his step. "You were supposed to keep them separated," Calhoun said to Last. "Another harebrained idea."

"Now she's living here," Archer said. "And by the look on Fannin's face, nothing could have made him happier."

Last sat mutinously on the couch, staring at his brothers. "I didn't know Mimi was going to have a stress attack of epic proportions."

"I didn't know Mimi was so lonely," Navarro said. "I feel pretty bad about that."

"Yeah." Last mulled that one for a moment. Alone most of the time, pregnant and with a sick father, Mimi was overtired, the doctor had said. He'd put her on total bed rest until the baby arrived. Which had Mason totally gonzo. He was turning into a protective bull right before their eyes—sending his precious Helga next door was the least he intended to do for Mimi.

But Kelly living at the ranch was far worse.

"What was that?" Last said, sitting up straight. "I heard a door slam."

"I heard it, too," Navarro said. "It came from upstairs."

They all listened.

And then they heard it, plain as paint on a fence.

Squeak, squeak, squeak!

Last sighed. "Bedsprings locked into the rhythm of love. I didn't even know Frisco's old bed had bedsprings in it. I think you can call that a very bad sign indeed."

"I don't think much housekeeping's gonna get done around here," Calhoun said.

"I'm hungry," Navarro stated.

"Think the kitchen's closed," Archer pointed out. "Yep, I think the only one of us around here that's going to be happy for a while is Fannin."

"Well, we did criticize his form with women," Last said.

"You're not making me feel better." Navarro got up and peered into the kitchen. "Anybody for toast?"

"Hell, no. I'm not staying here listening to that."

Archer put his hat on. "I'm going into town to get a burger at Lampy's."

His three brothers beat him to the door.

"I WAS MAD," Kelly admitted, lying breathlessly on a bed in some room she'd never imagined she'd first view from her back. Something had happened between her and Fannin as she went upstairs—all the anger she was holding inside somehow uncorked when he grabbed her hand and kissed her. "I think I didn't plan on having mad sex, though."

"Neither did I," Fannin said. "I hope your mood swings are always so productive."

She tossed a pillow at him, which he ducked. "I like you," he said. "You're playful."

He was so confident, it was annoying. "You know, you don't always get everything you want, Fannin Jefferson, just because you want it."

"I got you, didn't I?" he said smugly.

She tossed the last pillow at him, but he dodged it, laughing as he left the room. "Okay, now I'm really mad," she said to herself. "Now I see that there are shades to anger that I never imagined."

Still, she had to admit that Fannin was an awesome lover. She'd liked being ambushed by him! No man had ever pursued her with Fannin's focus, and therein lay his charm.

However, he'd be more charming if he wasn't such an ass, she thought, pulling her skirt down and fixing her hair. It had been so much fun to let herself go....

But he *was* an ass, and there was nothing in him that could become marriage material. Maybe she really was a good girl having a fling before settling down.

"It was fun, but that's it," she told Joy, who was napping in the window ledge, totally unconcerned with anything except her own sleep. "That's the last time the cowboy ambushes me." She wasn't putting a lot of time into a man who had no heart, fired old ladies and was overcocky. He would always make her mad, and after her parents' fiery relationship, she wanted something settled. Something secure.

Something she'd never have with Fannin.

She was not going to be his flame.

FANNIN FELT better than he ever had. He was going to get to keep Kelly for the next three days! And he wouldn't even have to admit that he didn't want her to go. That was in line with his brothers' modus operandi—say little and make 'em wonder.

He was happy Mimi felt better, but everybody was more comfortable with the new arrangements, he was certain. Mason had already carried Helga's stuff over to Mimi's, and Mimi was happily laid up in bed, lapping up Helga's attention like a lazy cat.

And he planned on having Kelly for breakfast, lunch and dinner.

Three days. Then it was Christmas, and Kelly would return home. With Helga. Kelly had made it clear that this year her mother and she were spending Christmas together in their home. One last time, as Kelly told him, because after Christmas she planned to tell her mother that she was going to Ireland for a very extended stay. It was time to live in her father's house and experience life through the things he'd left her.

Mason had been very understanding. By that time, Julia could have someone suitable sent over from the Honey-Do Agency to stay with Mimi until Helga returned. It was all going to work out so well.

"You see," Fannin told Bloodthirsty Black, "my brothers were obviously right. Storming. Conquering. That's the way to a woman's heart. It's all about handling a woman *right.*"

"YOU SEE," Kelly told Julia on the phone, "it's all about handling a man right. Why didn't I realize it was so easy?"

"I don't know. You never met anyone you liked before. So the Jefferson men aren't as bad as I imagined?"

"Nothing a little sweetness can't cure."

Julia laughed. "Maybe I'll take the job at Mimi's. I haven't spent time with my friend in ages."

Kelly gasped. "Why don't you do that? Mimi would be so thrilled!"

"And I might catch me a man, too," Julia teased. "Like you did."

"I don't know." Kelly scrunched up her nose. "I think the Jefferson men think women are for entertainment and amusement if nothing's on TV."

"You're pretty happy with the arrangement."

"Yes," Kelly said, "but it's not marriage. It would never be marriage with Fannin. I'm planning to meet my dream man in Ireland. That would be a fairy tale come true, wouldn't it?"

"Maybe you're already in love," Julia said.

"If you meet Fannin, you'll understand that he's capable of making me many things, but a wife is not one of them."

Chapter Seven

"Run that part past me again about the midwife," Mason said to Fannin the morning after the Mimi episode. "Because I'm not sure I understood."

"There's a lot going on we don't understand," Fannin said. "Some mysteries are too deep to be probed by the masculine mind."

The two brothers sat in the kitchen, waiting for Kelly to come down and fix their breakfast.

Only, she hadn't.

What they found instead was a note that said, "Gone to Mimi's. Help yourselves to the fridge."

Everyone else had lit out for town on a doughnut run.

Mason flicked the note disdainfully. "I do not like my routine messed with."

"It does kind of stink like roadkill." Fannin sighed. "I was hoping to have a pretty face pouring me coffee for a change."

He was fairly certain Kelly had deserted them to a meager breakfast out of spite. She seemed to know he was the one selected to get rid of her mother—and he was pretty certain she was going to hold it against him.

Or she was mad that he'd swept her off her feet last night. But that couldn't be it. She'd been way too enthusiastic.

Dang, he liked his women strong.

He also liked his breakfast hot and served. He traded frowns with Mason. "Maybe somebody should mention to Kelly what we like."

Mason shrugged. "To what purpose? She seems to have a pretty hot temper on her. We could end up with no dinner, too."

Mason was the only one of his brothers who didn't believe in storming the gates. Which was why he'd ended up without his true love, Fannin thought sourly. *He* wasn't going to end up like Mason.

"Now, look. Kelly is a Honey-Do employee, and we're paying for her service, and if we want breakfast, we should just say we want a hot breakfast every morning before we go outside and work our butts off in the cold!" Fannin stated.

The front door opened and Kelly entered, bright and cheery with wind-reddened cheeks. "Good morning," she said, looking into the kitchen. "It's cold outside."

Fannin slammed his mug down. "Damn right it's cold outside, woman! Do you think we should have to go out and work in twenty-degree weather with empty stomachs?"

She blinked. "Why, no, Fannin, I don't think you should at all." And then she smiled. "I'll be upstairs if you need me. Just bellow. As is your custom, apparently."

Kelly left, and Fannin stared at Mason. "What just happened?"

"You nicely got told to shut the hell up and fix your own breakfast, mice brains," Mason said. "Didn't you read her body language? Her widened eyes? The smirk she could barely contain? Those were all negative signals. Don't-mess-with-me-or-there'll-be-no-dinner signs."

"If you read women's bodies so well, then why—"

"Ah-ah-ah," Mason said, wagging his finger. "Let's not go there. You're already in trouble with the help. Don't add me to the list."

Fannin sighed, getting up to pour them both some lukewarm coffee. "All right. Back to the midwife question. Mimi wants a midwife because she doesn't want to go to a hospital. She found one she liked, only then that woman went to stay with her sister in Iowa. Mimi's spent so much time in a hospital with her father that she's spooked. And she says her mother had her at home, and our mother had all of us here, and we all lived to tell the tale. So she's going to have a midwife."

Mason shook his head. "I really don't want to be within twenty miles when she has the baby."

"Why?" Fannin stared at his brother, sensing more was going on than his usual thickheadedness.

"Because she'll be in pain and I don't want to hear that. I want it all antiseptic and clean and wrapped up nice and neat by professional hands—"

"Mason," Fannin said slowly, "you're a chicken liver."

Mason thumped his mug down, his eyes squinted dangerously. "How's that, Fannin?"

"You want Mimi to go to the hospital and have it all tidied up so you don't have to deal with it. You can just mosey in to the hospital with a cheap flower basket when it's all over."

"It's healthier for Mimi and the baby, knucklehead. Quit trying to go scientific on me."

"Psychological."

"Same thing. Last runs the psych ward in our house, okay? Even he thinks Mimi should have her baby around trained professionals."

"Listen." Fannin leaned in close. "I don't think you've realized it yet, but we're surrounded by the enemy. They've infiltrated our house, they're in cahoots and they're calling the shots with this baby thing. I wouldn't make too many comments about trained professionals."

"This from the man who won't fix his own breakfast." Mason drank from his mug. "It's just healthier in case there's a problem."

Fannin tapped the table.

Boom! Boom! Boom!

The brothers stared up at the ceiling.

"What…was that?" Mason asked.

"It sounded like she was listening to our conversation through the ceiling and giving us grief."

Mason shook his head. "You know, you picked quite a firecracker for a girlfriend."

"Who says she's my girlfriend?"

"Last."

Fannin grimaced. "Don't tell Kelly."

"Take my advice." Mason glanced away for just a moment. "If you like this girl, do something about it. Don't wait around."

Fannin waited.

But that was all Mason had to say. He got up and left the room after pouring his coffee into the sink.

Fannin sighed, going upstairs to find the cause of the banging. There were rustling sounds coming from inside Mason's room, which was odd, because Mason had gone out the front door. No one was in the house except Fannin and Kelly.

Quietly he approached the room.

Kelly was on top of a ladder, cleaning out the light fixture. The ladder was off balance because she'd propped it with two legs on the carpet and two off, so Fannin moved forward to steady it. "So you're the boom, boom, boom."

"I beg your pardon?"

"Nothing. Be careful."

"I'm fine."

"Just so." Fannin held the ladder, his eyes level

with Kelly's thighs. No, he told himself, now is not the time to think about her that way. She's cleaning a light fixture, and people don't have fantasies during a fixture cleaning. "Hey, I can do that."

"No, you can't," Kelly replied, not even halting in what she was doing.

"I can."

"No, you can't, Fannin. First of all, you're supposed to be outside working in the twenty-degree weather you mentioned. Secondly, Mama said not to let any of you boys do anything because you make twice as much work when you try to help."

"Ouch."

She looked down at him with those blue eyes, her cinnamon hair falling over one shoulder, and he wondered how he'd ever thought he wanted petite.

"Fannin, did you make extra work for my mother?"

"Well," he said, "do I get points if I say no?"

"You get nothing for lying."

"Oh. Well, I'm sure it wasn't intentional, but most likely we all did."

She sniffed and went back to what she was doing.

"That didn't sound encouraging. Did I get a point?"

"No. You totaled in the negative column by evading the answer and selling out your brothers in the same breath."

"Oh." He returned to staring at her dress, which stretched nicely across her thighs and other areas. A fantasy of tossing her dress up and giving her something she'd never forget crossed his mind and set his jeans afire.

He glanced up and she was looking down at him, her expression unsmiling and intent.

"Don't you even think about it," she said.

"What?" he asked innocently.

"Storming my portal."

He blinked. "Would I do that?"

"Yes. There's nothing under there but tidy whities."

"I'm not picky."

"I know." Her voice was a trifle more ironic than he liked. "But I've had my fling."

"I hate past tense. Did I ever tell you, I live totally in the present?"

She got down off the ladder and pulled a list from her pocket, ignoring him.

His method wasn't working. He scrambled for what his brothers would do now.

Leave her.

He didn't want to.

"Kelly, maybe we got off on the wrong foot."

She gave him an arched brow. "No, I'm perfectly coordinated. Thank you for your opinion, though."

Checking off her list, she left the room.

Fannin was left holding the ladder. "You *are* going to be mine," he said. "You just don't know it yet."

KELLY WORKED ALL DAY, going down the list carefully as her mother had requested. She even made dinner, though knowing now what she knew about the men not liking her mother's cooking, she overcame her stubbornness and went all out.

"Whoa, pot roast," Mason said as he sat down to his plate. Steaming potatoes, carrots and mushrooms surrounded the big chunk of gravy-covered meat.

Rolls and butter were passed around. Hot tea was in steaming mugs, which the men seemed to appreciate as they warmed their cold hands.

Fannin sat eyeing his plate. There was a bowl of Frosted Flakes in cold milk.

If he's smart, Kelly thought, he'll eat the breakfast he so dearly wanted without a word.

He ate it.

There wasn't even a hint of a comment from the Jefferson peanut gallery.

Kelly kept her eyes down as she refilled mugs with hot tea. More hot rolls were placed in a napkin-covered basket and passed around.

Fannin ate every bite of his cereal.

He looked so sad Kelly finally took pity on him. She'd made her point.

She fixed a heaping plate of meat, potatoes, and an extra roll. Silently, she placed a tea mug beside his plate, removing the cereal bowl.

She could feel his brothers taking in every move she made.

Fannin's hand shot out, grabbing her wrist.

Startled, she looked at him.

"This is the best meal I've had in years," he said, and Kelly's heart woke up, beating extra hard. Their eyes met, and she wished she could forget what had happened between them sexually. But she couldn't.

All she knew was that this man made her feel the way no one else in her life could.

"You're welcome," she murmured.

Nodding, he returned to eating.

The brothers hurriedly tucked in to their own dinners.

Kelly hesitated, her body on fire.

"You know what," she said suddenly, "I just remembered I'm spending the night with Mama at Mimi's. Do you gentlemen mind cleaning—"

"No, no," they all chorused. "You go on. We want to sit here and enjoy this dinner," Mason said.

Fannin looked up at her but she wouldn't meet his gaze. Untying her apron with swift fingers, she said, "Are you sure you don't mind? Because I—"

"Go on," Mason said, rising to walk her out.

"Sit down. Please." Kelly hurried to the door. "Everyone stay seated and enjoy your dinner. I'll be back in the morning."

She left, escaping into the cold without her coat. It was a fast jaunt over to Mimi's, and she couldn't have stayed another moment in that house with Fannin. He was making her feel things she didn't want to feel! Now was not the time to get obsessive over a man— she wanted to find her dream man in Ireland.

Not here in Texas, where she'd lived forever.

Suddenly, fast-walking boots overtook her, and she was swept off her feet.

"Fannin!" she said with a gasp. "You scared me!"

"Not as much as you should be scared," he said with a growl, burying his face in her hair as he walked. He found her neck and kissed it. Then she slid out of his arms, turning so that his kisses landed on her mouth instead. She moaned, trying not to lose her sanity, but he was so warm and wanting that she needed to stay near his fire.

"Oh my," she said as his hands roamed up her body. "Fannin—"

"I don't like it when you walk away," he said into her mouth. "I don't like it when you leave a room I'm in."

"Are you proposing I sit like a statue in one place?" she asked, wondering why his possessiveness didn't rankle her.

"A nude statue, if I have my way."

Somehow, her dress was going up and her hands were undoing his belt. It was pitch-dark outside, courtesy of wintertime, but still she worried. "Fannin, if my mother saw me kissing you, she'd—"

"Come on." He dragged her into a barn, fifty feet too far for her raging desire.

"Thank heavens for barns," she said, gasping as he pulled her inside the warmth.

"That's what we build 'em for."

She giggled as her dress hit the hay. "Not true."

"Totally true. Why do you think silos are shaped the way they are? It's male advertising. The bigger your silo, the bigger your—"

"Fannin!" She followed her dress to the hay, because he gave her a slight push, giggling as she went down.

"I have a *really big* silo."

"Stop. Let me take off my panties." But she was laughing, and she didn't want him to stop what he was doing to her. He kissed her mouth hard, then pushed aside her thong to get inside her. His tongue was sweeping the breath from her mouth, and all her giggles exploded into a screaming climax that had tears pouring from her eyes. Grabbing his shoulders, she pulled him to her with all her strength, burying him deep inside her.

"Did you say stop?" he asked, staring down at her, his eyes lit with mischief.

"No," she lied.

"I could have sworn—"

Squealing at his torture, she rocked against him instead, doing what she wanted to get what she needed. The pleasure hit her again, twice as wonderfully because he collapsed, gasping, at the same time.

"*Now* you can stop," she said smugly.

"You think?"

"I think."

He didn't move for a moment. Then he withdrew **and flipped** her onto her stomach. She felt hot man cover her nudeness as he snapped the back of her thong.

"You fibbed about the tidy whities," he said in her ear, "you bad girl."

She laughed, unable to help herself. "You didn't believe me in the first place."

"Yes, I did. I'm very gullible. And now you'll have to make up for your fibbing."

She took his hands and snuggled her face into them. "Gullible? I don't think so."

"Yeah. I am."

He popped her rear with the flat of his hand.

"Fannin!" she gasped.

"Yes?"

"What do you think you're doing?"

"Something I wanted to do from the moment I met you."

And then he slid inside her again. She screamed into his hand, loving every moment of the sweet torture.

"I like my breakfast hot and my dinner hot, but as long as you're as hot as you are for me, I'll eat every meal cold if that makes you happy," he said huskily into her ear. "If you're cooking it, it's going to be delicious, anyway."

She closed her eyes, passion and wonder flaring inside her at the spell of his words.

"I'm so glad you came to town," he told her, rocking against her so that she felt every thrust. "You're just right for me."

Then he lay still against her, though his cheek was against her back, and she could feel his heart beating against her shoulder. Gently he stroked her hair.

She loved every second of his attention.

"I'm in big trouble," Kelly murmured.

"What?" Fannin said, his words a sleepy grunt.

"Nothing," she said. "Nothing at all." She tried squirming out from underneath him, to no avail. "This has got to stop."

"Hang on," he said, suddenly sounding very awake. "Don't move."

That definitely had to cease. He could not go on being macho man. "Listen, buster, I'll move when I want to—"

He held her tightly still, his muscles tensed.

"What's wrong?" Oh, heavens, what if her mother was nearby? What would Helga say about her rolling around in a barn with a Jefferson brother?

"I think something just gave out," he said.

Chapter Eight

Kelly sat up as soon as Fannin released his strangle-hold on her. It wasn't doing any good anyway, because she'd struggled like a wary kitten in his arms.

"What do you mean something just gave out?" she demanded, sitting up to push tousled hair out of her eyes.

He took care of matters the best he could, grabbing his own clothes and handing her dress to her. "I mean the condom malfunctioned. It's all that body heat you give off. You melted it."

She gasped with outrage. "*I* melted it? *You* melted it, with your…your—" Her blue eyes were wide open. "Oh, no. I mean, you don't think—"

"I don't think so." He buckled his belt. "They were the best brand the pharmacy had. None of them advertise their record as far as not breaking."

"It should have been fine," Kelly said. "When did you buy them? A year ago?"

"Yesterday. Latex shouldn't give out in a day. I think it was a defect."

She went totally still. "Yesterday?"

"Yeah. You would have thought we'd be safe. I mean, the expiration date was still wet on the box." He winked at her. "I'm kidding. But they *should* put an expiration date on the box. They're like rubber bands and you know how those lose their snap."

She ignored his theory. "You bought condoms *yesterday*."

He hesitated at the change in her tone. "Yes."

"So this was premeditated."

"I don't meditate around you, Kelly. That's one thing I definitely don't do. I do not feel like going ahhmmmmm—"

She bounced out of the barn.

"Hey! I hate it when you do that!" He went after her, standing in front of her so she had to look at him. "Could we just finish one conversation to both our satisfactions?"

"I should have listened to my mother," she said. "You are all as wild as March hares."

"I don't understand why you're mad." He really didn't. But he wanted to understand so he could fix it. There was a major communication gap going on, and after sex he liked his women cooing and soft rather than howling mad. "Is it because the condom tore?"

Kelly stared at him. "I do not want to hear that verb in conjunction with condom again."

"Kelly, I'm sorry. Next time—"

"There isn't going to be a next time, Fannin," she

said. "This has got to stop now. Before you derail all my plans, all my dreams. Listen, you might think I'm made-to-order for you, but you're the absolute worst thing that could happen to me."

"That's a little harsh, don't you think?"

"I do not. And I cannot believe you bought condoms yesterday."

"Biggest box they had." He was genuinely confused. "Kelly, spell it out for me. What are you so angry about?"

"You presumed."

He rubbed the back of his neck. "Presumed we'd want safe sex?"

"Presumed we'd have sex!"

"Well, we already had, it was a given that we would again. I mean, I want to, and you seem happy."

Silence met that.

"You are, aren't you? Happy with me? I mean, you're not exactly putting up a fight. I didn't have to drag you in here like a caveman. My brothers are all about the caveman thing, but I go for subtlety." Fannin was proud of that.

Kelly shook her head and left the barn.

Fannin waited.

"Just for the record," she said, coming back inside, "I'm not ever doing that again. I'd be in big trouble if I got pregnant."

"Why?"

"Because we're all wrong for each other. We have

different life goals. We have nothing in common. My mother doesn't like you. You don't like her."

"I don't have anything against Helga. Not exactly. Not personally, anyway."

"It doesn't matter now, Fannin."

She left again.

He grinned. She was wrong. Great sex was the common denominator that leveled the playing field.

And the field was definitely level.

KELLY WENT STRAIGHT to Mimi's house, with only a glance back toward the barn. Fannin stood in the doorway, his silhouette clear from the light overhead. He was watching her, making sure she made it in safely.

A shiver rolled over her skin. He was so possessive, he made her nervous. She wasn't sure why she liked being the object of his sole attention. His focus unnerved her, scared her and yet made her feel very sexy.

She had never imagined trying not to fall in love could be such torture.

Mimi lay on a sofa in the sheriff's huge television room. Kelly entered the room quietly, thinking Mimi was asleep, but then Kelly realized Mimi was sobbing.

"Mimi!" Kelly said. "What's wrong? Are you hurting?"

Mimi wiped at her eyes with a tissue. "No. I feel much better."

"Are you having another panic attack? Isn't that what you called it yesterday?"

Mimi nodded. "I think maybe I am." She tossed the wet tissue into the trash and got another. "I do not understand why I'm constantly teary. This should be the happiest time of my life."

Kelly wasn't sure about that. Mimi was huge for such a petite woman. She looked like she was one minute from liftoff. "It's going to be okay, Mimi," Kelly said, reaching to comfort her. "Mama's here, and I'm going to be here at night when I get done working at the Jeffersons."

"Don't let them suck you in," Mimi said, blowing her nose so hard that the tissue flew around her fingers.

"Suck...me in?"

"Yeah. Don't fall for them. It'll happen before you realize it. One minute you're sitting on a log, and the next minute you're drowning in the swamp."

"I see," Kelly said, not really understanding but recognizing the words as a warning. Her skin went chilly.

"I shouldn't talk about them like that. I've known those boys all my life. We've been through everything together. But they're such *boys*. It's like they drank from Peter Pan's Elixir of Boyhood. And for some reason, women are attracted to that like bees to sugar water."

"Women like boys?"

"Yes." Mimi lowered her voice. "I haven't quite

decided if it's the mothering factor or the insipid desire to change them. It can't be done, you know. They can't be changed.'' Mimi sniffled.

"Um, do you think you could sleep now?'' Kelly asked, desperately wanting the subject changed. She wondered if she'd fallen into the Jefferson swamp. And if she had, which scenario was she subconsciously reacting to?

"I know four of them got caught,'' Mimi said. "But that was weird science. I mean, you wouldn't believe what the men put those girls through before they got to the altar. Frisco Joe, Laredo, Ranger and, ugh, I don't even want to talk about Tex. There's no simple romance with them.''

"Mimi, are you warning me about something specific?''

Mimi turned bright eyes on her. "I think I'm a little jealous that you're over there all day, alone in the house with Mason.''

"Mason?'' Kelly stared at her. "Oh…no, Mimi, you're not in love with Mason, are you? I mean—'' Her gaze swept Mimi's huge belly. And then she fell silent.

"He doesn't know,'' Mimi said. "And he never will. You mustn't tell a soul. It's so wrong of me to feel this way! I thought once I married Brian, somehow I wouldn't care as much. I'd get busy with the baby and some mom clubs…but it hasn't worked.''

Kelly's heart stung for Mimi. "I am so sorry. I had no idea.''

"Julia never told you?"

"Of course not. Julia would never gossip. When she sent my mother out there, she just said Helga was perfect for what the Jeffersons needed."

"It was perfect for what *I* needed. Which was keeping Mason mine. Is that not the most horrid thing you ever heard? I'm a horrid, horrid woman! And my child is going to have a horrid mother!"

"Oh, Mimi." Kelly didn't know what to say. She'd hate to be in love with a man she couldn't have. Instantly she thought of Fannin. Never again, she told herself. I'm staying out of that swamp! "Mimi, where's your husband?"

"In Austin. Or Houston. Depends on the case."

"Oh." That didn't help matters.

"Can I tell you a secret?"

Kelly nodded, not really wanting to hear it but realizing that talking was keeping Mimi from crying.

"We got married because of my father."

Kelly blinked.

"Because Dad was so sick and I was scared he wasn't going to last forever, and I wanted him to hold his first grandchild. And Brian agreed to…be the father."

Kelly's eyes widened. "Brian agreed?"

Mimi nodded.

"So you have a marriage of convenience?"

"We have a marriage," Mimi said with finality. "And I have a grandchild for my father."

Kelly leaned back against the sofa. No wonder Mimi was so miserable.

"My mother left when I was very young. She's alive somewhere, probably moving from man to man." Mimi tossed the final tissue away, seeming stronger now. "It's always been just me and Dad."

Helga had never said anything to Kelly about wanting her to get married and start a family. Kelly had never had that urge—until now.

Thankfully, Fannin had pointed out the path she was on. Now that she knew she was having a safe fling—*had been* having a safe fling—she could move on to finding Mr. Right. "I understand completely," Kelly said.

"Well, I knew you would. You've been raised with a single parent. You understand how it feels to want to make them happy. Helga would adore a grand-child."

"Do you think so?"

"Absolutely. Why do you think she's over here all the time mothering me?" Mimi looked at her wryly. "She couldn't mother you, because you were busy working. So she mothered me."

"Oh, dear." Kelly felt her own panic rising inside her. "I'm moving to Ireland."

Mimi looked at her. "Oh, that will make your stalwart mother happy."

"What do you mean?"

"It means don't kid a kidder. We single-parent

children are all our parents have. We don't go off to live in foreign places.''

Kelly knew her mother would be heartbroken, that was true. But it was something she needed to do. ''I'll never know who I am if I don't go. I'll never understand the other part of me.''

''I don't want to understand the other part of me,'' Mimi said bitterly. ''I would shave my head before I got to know my mother.''

Helga certainly felt animosity toward Kelly's father, which was to be expected since he'd abandoned them. ''But it's a ring house in Ireland,'' she murmured.

''Doesn't matter if it's a castle. Your mom will miss you. She doesn't complain, probably because she doesn't have the English to do it, but she's lonely here. Think about it. How would you like to be responsible for a ranchful of men who were really little boys?''

''Mason doesn't quite strike me that way,'' Kelly said.

''You're not going to fall for him, are you?''

''Absolutely not,'' Kelly said. ''I'm not going to fall for any of them.''

''Oh, boy,'' Mimi said, closing her eyes as she laid her head against the sofa. ''Famous last words. You know, eventually one of them will try to sleep with you. If you do not resist—at all costs—you'll be lost.''

Kelly's mouth dropped open.

"Of course, I never slept with Mason and I'm lost anyway." Mimi frowned. "Either way, you could be sunk."

"Do you think...Fannin drank from Peter Pan's Elixir of Boyhood?"

"Oh, he drank the big gulp," Mimi said. "He just disguises it under a kind and gentle demeanor."

"Kind and gentle demeanor? I haven't seen that side of him, except with my mother. And Joy."

"Who is upstairs comfortably sleeping on your mother's back."

"Back to Fannin and the big gulp—"

"Yes. Well," Mimi said, her voice lowered confidentially, "Fannin's lure is specific and targeted and all the worse because he won't *see* you once you fall for him."

"Spell that out for me slowly. I'm sort of a newbie where men are concerned."

"Okay. Fannin's sort of the honorable one among the brothers. He won't sleep with everyone he meets. He's very selective."

Which didn't make Kelly feel a whole lot better.

"So what happens is he's just really nice and treats everyone gently, which earns him a lot of grief from his brothers. Like if they're out with a group of women, everybody will sleep with someone that night except Fannin. He'll pick out the lonely girl and then spend all evening with her. And then she'll fall for him. But he won't sleep with her, at least not usually. He's had a girlfriend or two. One threatened to have his baby so he'd have to marry her. Whew," Mimi said. "I can tell you Fannin was out of there like his boots were on fire."

Kelly's stomach felt as if it was being iced.

"So Fannin's such a nice guy that the girls adore him, but he won't *see* them. You know, he never notices them."

"How do you know all this?"

"Oh," Mimi said with a slight laugh, "I know everything about those crazy men." She sobered for a second. "Which is a double-edged sword, because they know everything about me, too. It was fun growing up, because I'd sit around with them, listening to their stories, just being one of the guys. I knew what tricks they were pulling on whom...." She sat up. "It was a sword that later came back to cut me deeply. Once a man sees you as one of the boys he never considers you as a woman."

"Oh," Kelly said.

"Back to Fannin," Mimi said brightly. "He did have one girl we thought might be The One. She really brought out the animal in him. I think they made love in every hayloft in town."

"Oh," Kelly repeated, her insides knotting.

"She was mad for him. And it seemed he was crazy about her, too. You had to be careful what door you opened in case they were behind it nookying." Mimi giggled. "It seemed like she was perfect for him. Adoring, blond, petite."

"Oh, dear."

"Yeah." Mimi put a hand on her stomach. "And then one day, he was over it. Just like that. I never really knew what happened, but I heard that the girl mentioned the dreaded *M* word. Worse, the rumor mill mentioned that she wanted babies. Which is not something the brothers actually looked forward to at the time—there's twelve of them and they weren't hankering for more Jeffersons."

"Oh."

"I mean, marriage had to come up eventually," Mimi said practically. "She thought he was in love with her, the way she was with him. All that sweet charm really undid her."

"About that sweet charm. I don't really think I've seen that side of Fannin. I would call him more pig-headed than charming."

"Oh. That." Mimi waved it off. "He's just grand-standing."

"Grandstanding?"

"Mmm." Mimi's eyes closed. "You know, I'm starting to get sleepy."

"Wait, Mimi, I know you need your rest but I have to know—"

Gentle snores greeted her words. "Thanks for that cliffhanger," Kelly said. What was grandstanding, anyway? Did that mean Fannin had a soft inner core he was hiding under a tough layer of cock 'n' bull? To what purpose?

It didn't matter. She'd been warned. Fannin had elusive, sneaky charm, a huge sexual appetite, laser-like attention for his woman of the moment and a big gulp of Peter Pan Syndrome.

She wasn't going to end up like Mimi, eating from an old candy box of regrets.

Not everyone had a smart German mama to keep them out of trouble.

All the same, she knew she was feeling dangerous emotions that were new to her. What had Fannin said to her?

I'm so glad you came to town. You're just right for me.

He'd ordered a woman. Everything he wanted in a woman. She'd shown up, lonely and virginal and on the precipice of changing her life. The very type Mimi said Fannin was drawn to.

But not for long.

Not forever.

Chapter Nine

"Mama and I will leave tonight," Kelly told Mason the next morning. It was Christmas Eve, and they'd stayed as long as Kelly felt they could. Mimi would be fine, she told herself. She'd have a midwife and the Jefferson brothers to help her.

Helga was reluctant, but she wanted to see her own house and things again. It had been a long time since she'd had a vacation from the ranch.

"We'll manage without you," Mason said. "We understand wanting to be home for Christmas."

The other brothers at the table didn't say a word. Kelly knew they were so happy Helga had moved next door that they didn't care what they did without a housekeeper.

"If you put your luggage on the porch, I'll load it into your car," Fannin said.

"I don't have much, since I was only expecting to stay a day." She blushed uncomfortably, aware of all the brothers' gazes on her. "My mom won't take much, either, since we'll only be gone a few days. But thanks."

He went back to eating his breakfast. Hot this time, just the way he requested. Under normal circumstances, she would have made his breakfast so hot that it was burned, just to spite him for instructing her last night as if she was some kind of ready-made wife. But she didn't want him saying anything to her at all.

He watched her, waiting. Her skin flushed again. "I'll fix lunches for the fields. And then we'll be off. I don't like to drive in the dark...." *Ever since I ran over that deer,* she started to say, but then that brought back memories of making love on the seat of Fannin's truck, so she silently left the room.

The brothers stared at each other for a moment.

"Did she seem odd to you?" Mason asked his brothers.

They all shrugged.

"Maybe a bit quiet," Archer said.

"Could be tired," Last said.

"Probably PMS," Bandera offered.

"PMS?" Calhoun repeated. "What the hell is that?"

"I dunno. I heard it on some talk show one day. Maybe Oprah. Anyway, during specific times of the month, a woman gets PMS, which is short for Preliminary Monthly Shock. It changes her personality."

"Eww," Last said. "That was more info than I needed. Please spare my sensitive ears."

Fannin's attention was riveted. "So you think she might be…you know?"

"It's a chick thing, dude. Don't ask me," Bandera said. "You now know what I know."

"I know we'd better freaking lay low if she's…you know, monthly and all," Crockett said.

Navarro winced. "This would be a new thing in our house. Mimi was monthly all the time, I think, or else we never noticed."

"I think we'd notice," Archer said. "Shoeshine Johnson once said that his wife got out the shotgun when she had PMS and nailed the barn door with about five shots. Said she needed a stress reliever and they were out of whiskey."

"Jesus." There was a scraping sound upstairs, like furniture being dragged. Every man's eyes looked to the ceiling.

"This will definitely be a new experience for us," Mason said. "Alarming and new."

"You know what? I'm not hungry anymore." Bandera stood, tossing his fork to the table. "Somebody eat mine. I'm going on a doughnut run."

Everybody except Mason and Fannin jumped to their feet.

Another scrape sounded upstairs.

Mason glanced at Fannin. "Kelly doesn't seem to like you very much," Mason said. "Maybe you better go for doughnuts, too."

Fannin grunted. If Kelly was having a monthly issue, that was a great thing—no dividend from the condom that didn't live up to its billing. He wouldn't have minded, but she sure would have.

On the other hand, he wouldn't miss a chance to say goodbye to her. He might never see her again.

There was something to be said for ordering a girlfriend. Frowning, he admitted that he didn't want Kelly to leave.

"Are ya coming?" Archer demanded. "Or are you gonna stand there with your boots stuck to the floor?"

His brothers waited impatiently.

"I'm thinking."

"Don't. All the iced doughnuts will be gone," Calhoun warned.

"Man, look. This is dangerous territory," Bandera proclaimed. "If you need a tissue for your issue, to quote Austin Powers, get one. If not, how 'bout we get our asses on the road already, quoth myself?"

He might never see her again. "I'm staying."

"Your life is in your hands, bro," Last said.

Mason got up and grabbed his hat. "And with that, I think I'll hit the fields."

The front door slammed, leaving Fannin alone in the house with Kelly. For a moment he listened to the silence. Kelly had decorated the mantel with a wreath and stockings. She'd dragged a scrawny tree in from the field—he'd seen her ax its small trunk himself. He'd been watching her from afar, wondering what she was up to. He would have offered to help, but he sensed that, since their night in the barn, she didn't really want him around. She was so much like

Helga. Totally independent. Not needing a man to take down a Christmas tree for her. It was a small tree, true, but she'd decorated it with red ribbons and he could honestly say the house looked changed.

She didn't know the real him, and he didn't know nearly enough about her. Slowly he walked up the stairs. This time he was going to her minus the he-man cape he'd borrowed from his brothers. He was losing her anyway, so it didn't matter if he was himself. As Mason said, she wasn't all that keen on him.

And he didn't want to get his head blown into the next county by that PMS stuff.

"Kelly?" he called.

"Don't come in!" she hollered.

He halted outside Frisco Joe's old room, where Fannin and Kelly had once made quickie love. "Can I come in in a minute?"

"No!"

Great. It was his property, and he was denied. Taking a deep breath, he reminded himself about moody females. Like Princess, some women were not meant to be stormed. "I'd like to talk to you."

"Well, I can't right now."

He didn't like her snippy tone of voice. It challenged him, almost begging him to kick the door in. What was she doing in there, anyway, that was so necessary for secrecy?

"Go away, Fannin."

Go away, Fannin? He'd never heard that before from a woman. "Are you dressed?" he asked.

"Does it matter? You're not coming in."

His temper began to heat. "Maybe I am."

"No, you're really not because I pushed the bed in front of the door."

Hence the scraping sound. He didn't doubt that she had because she was a big, strong woman and he'd seen her take down a tree, albeit a small one, and drag it across a clearing. Closing his eyes, he counted to ten and told himself to wait for sanity. It would come back eventually. She just made him see shades of his personality he wasn't used to seeing—like *muy mal* temper.

"Fannin, I can hear you out there breathing. You sound like Darth Vader. This is one time you can't storm me, so go away. I'm busy. I need to leave in a couple hours and I must get this done."

He ground his teeth. It was the mothering tone she was using. Not like the one she used when he had her in his arms, squealing and moaning from pleasure.

Damn it, this tone he didn't care for. It was his house, and she was…not his woman, he told the red planet growing inside his head. Not, not, not. Remember the PMS thing. Remember you're a gentle man.

She was avoiding him. But not the real him. The manufactured, copycat-brother him.

"Kelly," he said, "if you don't open this door so that I can talk to you face-to-face, I'm going to behave like Jack Nicholson in *The Shining.*"

"The ax in the door thing?"

"Yes. My version of a fireman rescue."

"Oh. If you do, can you bring me a pair of scissors?"

Ooh. She might have just trumped him. He didn't care to meet his maker by way of scissors. "We don't have any," he lied.

"Fannin, you're such a fibber. There's three good, sharp pairs in the kitchen drawer and a pair of poultry scissors in the knife block."

She was acquainted with the inventory of the knife block, too. And he was alone in the house with her. "Hey, Kelly, how are you feeling today, by the way?"

"I feel like…not being pestered. You?"

"Same, I'm sure. Before you leave, maybe I could take you on a horse ride. Sort of a thank-you for everything you've done." Oh, boy, was that ever lame.

"I don't think so. Thanks."

He couldn't bear it another moment. Sanity had not yet returned, and he was beginning to think that it never would. Not with this woman. She played aloof far better than he did.

There was only one thing to do.

He was going to use Frisco Joe's method of entrance: the ladder/drain pipe trick, whichever one was still behind the crepe myrtles and sturdiest. He had every right to know what was going on in his own house. "Okay, maybe another time," he said, walking away, his boots thumping purposefully on the stairwell.

Around the house, he located the old ladder, left

just where Frisco Joe had hidden it to keep it away
from Helga's prying eyes. She had come to the ranch
when Frisco Joe had suffered a busted leg and had
decided to nurse Frisco Joe to the point that he was
convinced he was in a scene from *A Clockwork Orange*.

Of course, that was Frisco for you, all dramatic.
Helga wasn't that bad, though she'd seemed that way
in the beginning.

Well, she could be annoying at times. But he
wasn't totally opposed to her. "Now," Fannin said
with satisfaction, pulling the ladder from behind the
thin bushes and placing it quietly against the brick
wall. Stealthily, he climbed up, hoping Kelly
wouldn't hear him and pull the blinds.

When he made it to the top of the ladder, he held
his breath and peered over the ledge into the window.

Kelly sat in the middle of the room, surrounded by
what looked like hundreds of packages, boxes, wrapping paper rolls and fancy, elegant ribbons. She re-
sembled an elf or a fairy, with her nutmeg hair falling
down her back as she taped and cut precisely. Joy sat
atop a particularly large box, watching everything her
mistress did with nonsubtle doggie curiosity.

He'd never seen so many presents in his life. She
hadn't brought all those with her from her home in
Diamond, because he'd seen every inch of her car as
he'd cleaned the deer guts off of it. Where had all
that stuff come from?

Maybe her mother told her to wrap them. Maybe

The Harlequin Reader Service® — Here's how it works:

Accepting your 2 free books and gift places you under no obligation to buy anything. You may keep the books and gift and return the shipping statement marked "cancel." If you do not cancel, about a month later we'll send you 4 additional books and bill you just $3.99 each in the U.S., or $4.74 each in Canada, plus 25¢ shipping & handling per book and applicable taxes if any.* That's the complete price and — compared to cover prices of $4.75 each in the U.S. and $5.75 each in Canada — it's quite a bargain! You may cancel at any time, but if you choose to continue, every month we'll send you 4 more books, which you may either purchase at the discount price or return to us and cancel your subscription.

*Terms and prices subject to change without notice. Sales tax applicable in N.Y. Canadian residents will be charged applicable provincial taxes and GST.

PLAY Lucky 7

and get 2 FREE BOOKS and a FREE GIFT

Scratch off the gold area with a coin. Then check below to see the gifts you get!

NO COST! NO OBLIGATION TO BUY! NO PURCHASE NECESSARY!

YES! I have scratched off the gold area. Please send me the **2 FREE BOOKS AND GIFT** for which I qualify. I understand I am under no obligation to purchase any books as explained on the back of this card.

354 HDL DZ44   **154 HDL DZ5K**

FIRST NAME   LAST NAME

ADDRESS

APT.#   CITY

STATE/PROV.   ZIP/POSTAL CODE   (H-AR-05/04)

7 7 7 — Worth **2 FREE BOOKS** plus a **FREE GIFT!**

Worth **2 FREE BOOKS!**

Worth **1 FREE BOOK!**

Try Again!

DETACH AND MAIL CARD TODAY!

they were Christmas presents from Helga. He gasped, suddenly realizing he hadn't bought a thing for the stalwart housekeeper. Maybe they were all for the baby...but then Kelly stood, counting, and he followed her finger as she counted to twelve.

They were for the brothers.

It looked like a winter wonderland in there.

Kelly put her head down, checking a list before writing on something. He watched her, suddenly struck by what the future could look like, if he was a lucky man, a man who pulled his head out of his butt in time to catch this woman and make her his wife. His family could grow up with this beautiful, talented, red-tressed amazon. His mouth went slack with the fantasy, and he began to feel something tugging at his jeans...tugging...tugging harder...

''Ch! Ch!''

Glancing down, he saw Helga—the housekeeper from hell—jerking at his jeans leg, her eyes blazing. ''Ch! Ch!''

''Damn it!'' He lost his grip, tumbling from the ladder, cussing. The last thing he thought as he hit the ground was that whatever he broke, he hoped Kelly would stay around to fix it.

The window above him flew open. Kelly stared down, a wicked angel grinning at him. ''Did you bring the scissors?''

''No. And thank heavens I wasn't looking for sympathy.''

''You're not dead,'' she pointed out. ''Your eyes

are open and nothing appears to be sticking out at a funny angle. I think you'll live.'' She slammed the window, but he heard her giggle before she did.

"She's cruel,'' he told Helga, who was staring down at him. "I think I'm in love with your daughter.''

"Ch. Ch,'' she said, clearly still annoyed and not even trying to understand him.

Then she walked away.

"Oh, God,'' he said, "like daughter, like mother. It could have been easier, couldn't it? I didn't need the Curse of the Broken Body Parts visited on me.'' Gingerly he sat up. "I think my spleen's ruptured.'' And his pride, but he wasn't going to dwell on that. Pride had got him to the top of that ladder and pride had brought him down off it.

Kelly appeared beside him, her poodle at her feet. "That's what you get for being such a little boy, sneaking to see your presents.'' She put a strong hand underneath him, which he welcomed, and helped him up. "My mother's so upset with you that I don't think you're going to get any presents.''

"She took ten years off my life. I won't get her a present, either.''

Kelly laughed. "Fannin, she didn't know I wouldn't let you in while I was wrapping presents, nor did she know that was the room I was wrapping in. She thought you were being a pervert. And she was protecting me.''

"Your mother thought I was a pervert?''

"She thought I was undressing and you were watching. Why else would a man be up a ladder? You clearly weren't washing the window. And she said you had a stupid expression on your face, like you were, you know, watching something really interesting."

"What makes her think I'd stoop to window-spying on her daughter?"

"I don't know. Of course, we've paired off in your truck, an abandoned bedroom and a barn, so maybe she's on to something. She probably senses you have some kind of lecherous thing going for me. Anyway, she says no woman is safe around any of you. Road to ruin and all that."

Great. He was never going to make Helga a mother-in-law if she thought he was a perv.

"We're sort of doomed as a couple, aren't we?"

She looked up at him as they walked, her eyes laughing. "I didn't think it was possible for my mother's opinion to be any lower of you. The ladder incident was a ringer, though."

"So, 'doomed'?"

"Yeah. *Doomed* is the word I'd use. How are you feeling?"

"Like not being pestered," he said, repeating her earlier words.

"I'll remember that when you're in the middle of something and I decide to spy on you. I'm never going to get all that stuff wrapped now, if I have to waste time with you."

She opened the front door, and he limped over to the easy chair. "I think I just got the breath knocked out of me. Feel free to go on with what you were doing. Don't let a frayed spine and a possible lateral rearrangement of my gluteus disturb you."

"Do you want me to call your brothers? Doc Gonzalez?"

"I'm fine." He felt like his bell had been rung, but from rodeo experience, he knew he was in good enough shape to live. "Sorry about that."

She stood at his arm, and he looked up into her blue eyes. "Fannin, I didn't want you to know I was wrapping your Christmas gifts from my mother. She wanted it to be a secret."

"I figured that out."

"She wanted me to leave them where you all would have a Santa-Claus-style surprise when you came downstairs tomorrow morning. She says she doesn't think any of you have had that in a long time. That was her real gift to you."

He grunted, touched beyond words but not wanting to say it.

"Of course you Jeffersons don't deserve it. You know that. I know that. My mother chooses to think of your mother and what she'd want for her children."

He closed his eyes. "Everything about you annoys the crap out of me somehow."

"Same." She giggled.

"Why does that feel so good?" he asked.

"I don't know. It's probably sicko magnetism or something."

"Like *Fatal Attraction?*"

"You watch a lot of movies, don't you?"

He grimaced. "Yeah."

"What can I get you before I go back upstairs? I still have a ton to do."

"The remote. I think I'll watch *It's a Wonderful Life.*"

"Now there was a man who tried to live right in spite of all the odds." She smiled and handed the remote to him. "Just ring a bell if you need me."

He got it. "Sure, angel. Whatever you say. Just as soon as you sprout wings. Right now, I consider you more of a red-haired devil."

"Well, here's a red-furred angel to make you feel better." She scooped Joy into his lap, and the tiny poodle settled in instantly. Kelly left the room, and he closed his eyes. His thoughts burned in his mind, greater than the pain he was suffering in his entire body.

She was going to drive him insane—if he wasn't there already.

"Merry Christmas," he said to Joy. "It's a *wonderful* life."

Chapter Ten

Fannin was annoyed, but he also recognized that he had some patching up to do. He doubted Helga thought he was an actual miscreant, but laziness she could attribute to him.

It was Christmas Eve, and he hadn't done a bit of shopping. Nor had any of his brothers, he was sure. He was suddenly stricken by the urge to get Kelly a Christmas present. Without disturbing Joy, who was napping in his lap, he swiped the portable phone.

"Union Junction Salon, this is—"

"The most beautiful girl on the planet," Fannin said.

"Hey, Jefferson wild man," Lily said with a giggle. "Which one are you?"

"One who needs a favor from his lovelies."

"Does this involve a Santa suit or elf leggings?"

Fannin laughed. "Neither. Just some shopping."

"We all love shopping. And some of us are available for a friend in need."

"Great. I'll meet you in thirty minutes."

"Where are we going shopping?"

"We'll need to go into Dallas."

"Oh, goody. I was hoping you'd say that. Bye, big guy."

"Bye, little lady." He punched the button to the phone with a grin. Kelly was standing at his elbow. She reached for Joy, but he stopped her with a hand. "What are you doing? Eavesdropping?"

"That would be the appropriate response from a woman who's been spied on," she said smartly. "But no, I wasn't. May I have my dog?"

"Not until you tell me how much of that you heard."

She eyed him. "Something about a little lady and thirty minutes."

He bit the inside of his mouth. If he didn't know better, he'd think flames were shooting out of his angel's ears. "Jealous?"

"Do I look jealous?"

"You look red-hot."

"Well, that's because you've just fallen off a ladder and your vision's distorted. May I have my dog, please?"

"Kelly, what time are you leaving?"

"As soon as you give me my dog," she said huffily.

Whoo-wee. Maybe the PMS factor was still in play. He'd have to ask his brothers how long that lasted. Surely not more than an hour or two. He squinted at her. "I was hoping you'd stay a little longer than thirty seconds." But he handed Joy to her, anyway.

"Well—"

The door burst open. "Kelly, your mother says to come quick!" Mason said. He was just in from the field and sweaty, with fear on his face. "She called me on my cell. She says she needs you to help her with Mimi. *Immediately*."

"I'll drive you over." Fannin hopped to his feet.

For once, Kelly didn't argue. She grabbed her purse, put Joy in it, and together they ran to his truck.

At the Cannady house, Kelly trotted up the stairs, leaving Fannin in the kitchen with Mason and Joy, who was eating out of a food bowl that had been placed there for her.

"What do you think is going on?" Fannin asked Mason.

"She said something about the baby. I don't think she could get through on the house phone, so she called me."

Fannin frowned. "I called the Union Junction ladies, but I was only on the phone for a second."

"With all of us having cell phones and hardly ever being in the house, I've never seen the need for call waiting, but at least she thought to call my cell."

Fannin nodded. "Maybe Mimi's having another panic attack."

"I don't know." Mason looked up at the ceiling. "I'll bet she never called Brian."

Fannin thought that was a pretty safe bet. But he

kept his mouth shut. He had enough problems with his own love life. Joy crunched contentedly on the tiny food in her bowl, and Fannin grinned at her. "When I come back in my next life, I'm gonna be a dog."

"Kelly would probably let you wear a collar if you wanted."

Fannin stared at his brother. "That was uncalled for."

"Sorry. Just happened to witness the downfall of Ladder Man while I was in the field."

Fannin's face burned. "Just trying to see if the sunlight was at such an angle to ruin the furniture in that room."

Mason laughed. "Did you see anything good?"

Fannin thought about all the gifts and Kelly sitting in the middle of them. "Yeah. I did."

"I should ask you not to play Peeping Tom on our guests."

"Okay," Fannin said. "I'll remember that."

"Until the next time," Mason filled in.

"Something like that."

"Damn it." Mason drummed the table. "You'd think they could give us a freaking update."

A moan came from upstairs. Fannin watched as his brother sat straight up in his chair, then went white as a Sunday shirt.

"You all right?" Fannin asked.

Mason ran a finger around his flannel shirt collar. "Yeah. I'm going to go home and take a fast shower.

Call me if you need me. But I'll be right back. I just don't want to sit in here stinking up the place. Or the hospital, in case we have to make a run for it.''

Fannin nodded, watching his brother leave. Good stiff outdoor air would put the color back in Mason's skin. He didn't blame his brother for taking off. "I'd like to do the same," he said to Joy, "but I don't guess I will. And that reminds me." Pulling his cell out of his pocket, he called the Union Junction Salon. "It's me. Going to have to take a rain check. Mimi's making noise upstairs. Could be the baby, could be something else. Think I'll hang around here, though."

"What exactly did you have on your Christmas wish list?"

Fannin rolled his eyes. "Everything. You name it. I've got eleven brothers, a housekeeper I really need to suck up to, a next-door neighbor moaning, a sick sheriff, and all of y'all. Plus a special lady friend."

"Oh," she said. "That sounds lucky for you."

"Not when you don't have a Christmas gift."

She laughed. "We're going into the city. We'll pick you up some things."

"You don't have to do that."

"But you'd sure appreciate it."

"Yeah." Fannin smiled. "I would, actually. But I hate to ask you to spend your Christmas Eve shopping for me."

"There are ten of us here. If we all grab a couple of things, it'll take an hour at most. Plus, we owe your family one."

"We owed you one after the big storm."

"And you got us this wonderful house for our salon after we had to leave Lonely Hearts Station. We're happy in Union Junction."

He grinned. "Lord only knows we all look better with our hair trimmed."

She laughed. "Talk to you later. Wish Mimi good luck for us if the baby's coming on Santa's sleigh."

"The way she sounded a moment ago, I think she wishes it *was* a sleigh."

"Hey, anything in particular for this lady friend?"

"I wouldn't know, to be truthful. Something for a tiny red poodle would probably not go amiss."

"Gotcha. You really are sucking up."

He chuckled.

"I'll see what I can do. 'Bye."

He hung up, and Joy jumped into his lap. Kelly came down the stairs, her eyes showing concern.

"What's going on?" Fannin asked. "Do you need me to do anything?"

"I don't know. She won't let us call Doc Gonzalez. Says it's Christmas Eve and she's just having Braxton-Hicks contractions. Warm-up contractions. Nothing to get excited about, she says, but I'm not so sure."

"How the hell does Mimi know what a Braxton-Hicks contraction is?"

Kelly shook her head. "I don't know. She says she took some classes and read a lot of books."

"Oh, that makes us all feel better. Did she call Brian?"

Kelly's gaze slid away. "I don't know."

"What is her problem about calling her husband?"

She looked down. "Fannin, I don't know, okay? Can we just get back to the basics?"

"I thought husbands were pretty basic, as in father of the child that's waiting to be born upstairs?"

"Don't snap at me!"

"I'm sorry. I'm just trying to make certain we're doing what needs to be done. Okay, if she won't let us call Doc or Brian, how about the midwife?"

Kelly swallowed. "She said she never had time to find another one."

"Great gravy." Fannin looked down at the little poodle in his lap, totally undisturbed by the household drama. "And no hospital."

"She says it would be a dry run, and she doesn't want to sit in a hospital on Christmas Eve. And she doesn't want to leave her father. She says we all need to calm down."

Mason burst through the door, his hair sopping wet, his clothes changed.

"You're going to catch pneumonia," Fannin told him.

"How's Mimi?" Mason demanded.

Fannin rubbed his eyes. "Intractable as always. Mason, why don't you go upstairs and see if you can ease some sense into Mimi's skull?"

He looked like he'd rather be shot. "Has anybody called her husband yet? I'm pretty sure we're getting close to needing him to start traveling from Houston.

I think he needs to be here. That's who should be putting sense into Mimi's head, if it could be done in the first place."

They all glanced at each other. Another moan floated down the stairwell.

"All right, so I'll go upstairs," Mason said reluctantly. "But have Brian on speed-dial in case I get the go-ahead for us to call him."

He went up the stairs. Fannin sighed.

"How long has Mason been in love with Mimi?" Kelly asked softly.

"I honestly do not know. It snuck up on him. Sort of like a bad rash when you've been in poison ivy."

Kelly sat at the table with him. "You don't always have to hold my dog."

"Yeah, I kinda do. She makes herself at home."

"Hand her to me."

"Nah." Fannin shook his head. "She likes my lap better."

Kelly smiled. "The novelty will soon wear off."

He looked at her. "Will it?"

He saw her catch her breath at his underlying meaning.

Then he went back to patting Joy and listening for Mason to holler if he needed him.

A FEW MOMENTS LATER, Mason returned looking, Kelly decided, as if he'd aged five years. "She's in pain but not letting on."

"All right." Fannin put Joy on the floor. "Here's

what we're going to do. I'll go make sure my truck is full of gas. Mason, you go ask the sheriff what he wants to do. He'd be better off at our house if Mimi won't leave this one. I just don't think it's good for him to lie up there listening to Mimi give birth to a baby.''

Instantly his cell phone rang. ''Yes, sir. All right, sir. Perfectly, sir.'' He hung up.

Mason looked at Fannin. ''Sheriff?''

''Yes. Apparently our voices carry quite acoustically up that stairwell,'' Fannin said, chagrined, his voice lowered.

''He tell you to get stuffed?''

''Pretty much.''

''Same thing he told me.'' Mason looked at Kelly. ''We're men of few words and repetitive phrases. 'Get stuffed' is pretty tame for a man who's more used to telling us to get—''

''And he also mentioned,'' Fannin interrupted, ''that the first person who tried to take him out of his own house where his grandchild was being born would see the wrong end of the shotgun he keeps under his bed.''

''Forgot about the shotgun,'' Mason said.

''They're so damn stubborn in this house,'' Fannin said. ''I do not understand how two people can be so danged stubborn.''

Kelly stared at Fannin, wondering when he'd last examined his own family tree and temperament.

''What?'' he said.

"Nothing. Please go on with your planning. It's the first sensible thing anyone's said since we got here." Actually, she was admiring his take-charge attitude. Fannin in full-blown maneuvering mode was pretty impressive.

"Okay. Since the sheriff's determined to be where his grandchild might be born, this is easier than the hospital anyway. We've got Helga to monitor the situation, and I feel pretty certain she can handle just about anything." Fannin looked at Kelly. "And we have you. Unless you're still going home."

"I wouldn't leave my mother on Christmas Eve," Kelly snapped.

"I didn't think so. What else do we need?"

"Brian and a doctor," Mason said.

"Did she tell you that you could call him?" Fannin asked.

"She didn't say I couldn't."

"You mean you didn't ask," Kelly said.

"I didn't ask," Mason admitted.

Fannin said, "I think we should call him," and looked at Kelly. "It's fricking Christmas Eve. Why isn't he here with his wife, anyway?"

"Don't look at me. I didn't know any of you until a couple of days ago. I'm just a bystander."

He sighed. "Hand me that phone book over there with all Mimi's scribblings in it."

Mason tossed it at him. Fannin found the name, then dialed the number.

"Hello?" a female voice said.

Fannin frowned. "May I speak to Brian, please?"

"He's taking a shower."

"Ah. I see." He looked at Kelly for support, but she and Mason were staring at him, completely unaware of what was being said. He was going to have to probe deeper. "It's important."

"Who is this?" she said.

"Fannin Jefferson of Union Junction, Texas. And who might I be speaking with?"

"I'm Mindy. Brian's girlfriend."

Fannin closed his eyes. "He can call me back if he wants to. Thanks." He switched the cell phone off, opening his eyes to see Mason and Kelly staring at him.

"Well?" Mason said.

How was he going to tell his brother that the suffering woman upstairs was on her own?

"Was he there?" Kelly asked. "Did you reach him?"

"I don't think so." Fannin got to his feet. "Think he's got other plans for the holidays. Look, we're all pretty much out of our league here. I say we tell Mimi she *has* to get to the hospital. This is not a calf we're talking about. It's a *baby*."

Kelly knew by the changed tone of Fannin's voice that something had gone wrong with the phone conversation. "I don't think she'll listen to me, guys. She barely knows me. I think it's going to have to be one of you who convinces her."

"That would be you, Mason. C'mon, Kelly. Help

me load the truck with whatever we might need to take Mimi into town to the hospital.''

''All right.'' Kelly thought Fannin had the best idea of any of them so far. ''Mason, please tell Mama I'll be right back.''

Mason's gaze rolled to the top of the stairwell. ''What did women do in medieval times? In Adam and Eve's time?''

''Mason, don't freak out here. It's a baby,'' Fannin said. ''We can handle this.''

''Fannin,'' Kelly said, ''be easy.''

''I'm trying to. But look at him. He's shaking like a leaf in a storm. I've never seen his hands tremble like that. Well, once before, but that was many years ago.''

Kelly looked up at him. ''Let's just go pack the truck.''

''Mason, we'll be right back.''

Mason nodded and slowly went up the stairs.

Fannin and Kelly looked at each other. ''I don't think he's with us,'' Kelly said. ''He acts like that's his baby being born.''

''Well, sometimes life is stranger than fiction. Come on.''

Chapter Eleven

Mason approached the stairwell, dreading each stair. By the look on Fannin's face when he'd called Brian, Mason knew with sickening clarity that something had gone terribly wrong. He didn't need further information to understand that Mimi was in trouble.

He walked into her room and took a seat next to her. Helga nodded at him and left the room, indicating she needed more ice and towels. Mimi turned to look at him.

"You're back," she said.

"Yeah."

"I feel calmer when you're here."

"Funny you don't have that same effect on me."

She tried a wry smile. "I never did."

"No." He stared at her, seeing her fragility for the first time. "Mimi, I want to take you to the hospital. You need to be examined by professionals."

Her eyes filled with tears. "I don't want to leave my father on Christmas Eve, Mason. What if it's his…last Christmas?" she said softly. "I would regret that forever, Mason. You of all people should understand that.''

Oh, boy. ''Okay, let me think, Mimi. Why won't you let me call Doc Gonzalez?''

''You can if you want to. I just don't think there's a need yet. I read that first babies can take a couple of days to arrive. Truly I'm not being stubborn. There's just nothing really happening yet. I have an occasional pain and that's it.''

She moaned and turned onto her side. He waited, helpless.

Moments later she rolled back over, her eyes closed. ''See? That's all that happens. I get a pain, it's a bit worse than a cramp, and then it goes. I really believe I'd be feeling more than that if the baby was on the way.'' Her eyes opened to meet his gaze. ''I'd go if it wasn't Christmas Eve, but I'm pretty sure this is nothing.''

Mason checked his watch to time the next nothing contraction. ''We couldn't get ahold of Brian.''

Her gaze didn't change. ''I didn't expect you to be able to. He has a big case he's working on.''

They stared at each other, and for a moment Mason thought he saw the old familiar belligerence in his friend's eyes. ''I'm going to be an uncle,'' Mason said. ''I can hardly believe it. My little Mimi, a mother.''

''I'm not your little Mimi, anyway. I'm big as a barn.''

''Yeah. But I kinda like your waddle.''

"You will pay when I am able to retaliate," Mimi told him with a smile. Then she rolled onto her side, hiding her face from him as another contraction hit.

Mason checked his watch. Five minutes.

"Damn it," Mimi moaned.

"What?" Mason demanded, his blood pressure elevating.

"I think I just wet the bed."

"Wet…the bed?"

"Mason, you have to leave now. Get Helga and ask her to bring fresh sheets."

Mason blinked. "No, Mimi. I'm taking you to the hospital *now.*"

"I won't go, Mason. I'm not leaving my father."

"We're going." He went to move her from the bed himself, but she was curled up into a tight ball and he had no idea how to move her. "You did wet the bed, tiger."

"Not funny, Mason. One day when you're incontinent, you'll hear that word again." Mimi blew breaths like she was blowing out birthday candles.

"Uncurl so I can lift you."

"No." She blew more breaths. "I don't feel like being jacked with, either, so get out."

Whew. Crabby. He thought that was a sign of imminent danger. "I'm calling Doc."

"I don't care what you do!" Mimi yelled.

Mason went into the hallway.

"Son," the sheriff said.

"Yes, sir?"

''Quit badgering my daughter.''

''I think she needs trained personnel, sir.''

''She wants to do it the way she was born. We didn't have all that fancy nonsense back then. Relax. It'll be fine.''

''Sir, she could have painkillers. She could have nurses, and people who know what they're doing.''

''You're just making her mad, Mason. She says she's not going. Have you ever known Mimi to change her mind?''

A squeal came from Mimi's bedroom. Mason's hair stood straight up. ''No, sir.''

''It's best not to fight with her right now, then. You gotta work with the cards you're dealt.''

He didn't want to play this particular game. Mason wanted someone else to deliver Mimi's child. He wanted to be a muss-free uncle. Antiseptic and next door. But they were tough, annoying country stock, and they were going to do it their way. Which he understood because he was the same way. ''Yes, sir,'' he said, and returned to Mimi's room.

Helga had the bed changed and Mimi in a fresh nightgown. Mason sat down in a chair by the window, looking at his friend.

It was a mistake. The whole thing was a comedy of errors. This should be his child. Mimi should be his wife.

But those thoughts were the wrong ones to have. The past couldn't be changed. Wasn't that what drove everybody on the planet? People made choices, and then they lived with those choices.

He closed his eyes and waited.

FANNIN AND KELLY WENT into the main house on the Jefferson property. All the brothers were perched in the den. "What's happening?" they demanded.

"Nothing yet," Fannin said. "Just some aches and pains. And some groaning."

"Mason's?" Archer wanted to know.

"Exactly. We need to get a truck ready for riding."

"Mason just called," Bandera said, "and he said not to knock yourself out. Mimi's definitely not leaving."

Fannin frowned. "That's a turn of events. He looked like he might drag her when we left."

"Nope," Bandera said. "Think we're in for some real drama."

Kelly sighed. "I'll make some hot tea for you while you wait. Anybody want some, before I go back over to help my mother?"

The brothers' expressions guiltily slid away from her.

"We can get it ourselves. Thanks, Kelly," Calhoun said.

Since when did this bunch not want to be waited on?

"Sit down, Kelly," Fannin said. "You're off duty for the holidays. We're hitting the restart button and taking care of ourselves for a few days."

She pursed her lips. ''Then I think I'll go upstairs and freshen up. If my mother calls, somebody please get me.''

Hurrying upstairs, Kelly unlocked the bedroom door—she'd swiped a key from Helga's hiding place as her mother instructed—and went inside. Almost everything was wrapped.

Everything except for her mother's present to Fannin. Pulling the blinds down so there'd be no repeat of the earlier incident—although she didn't think even Fannin would be so stupid, but you could never tell—she turned on a lamp that threw a soft glow into the room.

Kneeling, Kelly pulled a sweater out from underneath the bed. Her mother had knit the sweater, using deep shades of blue, green and red. It was a lovely sweater. Helga had explained that Fannin needed one because all of his had holes. Helga had been very touched when he offered to take her out to the movies, knowing he didn't usually go anywhere except maybe Lampy's or somewhere in town.

She didn't like him, she'd emphasized to Kelly. All of the boys were bad except Mason. But Fannin needed a new sweater. Smiling, Kelly placed the sweater in a box and wrapped it. She could understand why the men resented Helga's mothering—and she could understand why Helga was annoyed by the men. It was such a shame that the relationship hadn't worked out, because it was one with benefits on both sides.

A knock at the door had her shoving the present underneath the bed. "Yes?"

"Kelly, it's Last."

Her eyes widened. "Have you heard from Mason? Is it Mimi's baby? Does mother need me?"

"No. We'd like to talk to you for a minute. If you don't mind."

She frowned. "We?"

"Archer, Calhoun, Navarro, Bandera, Crockett and me," Last said.

That was quite a roll call. "Can I meet you downstairs?" She didn't want them anywhere near the presents.

"Sure."

Swiftly, she stuck a bow on Fannin's package, took a last mental count of everything her mother had asked her to do, then scooped up Joy. "Let's go see what those mean old men want."

Downstairs, she found the brothers in chairs, obviously waiting for her. Their hair was slicked, their shirts were straight. Not a boot was on a table. "You wanted to see me?"

They all stood. Kelly gasped. "Well, sit back down, you're making me nervous."

They sat, and she sat with Joy in her lap.

"Kelly," Last said. "We owe you an apology."

She blinked. "For?"

Last's ears turned a little pink. The other brothers shifted in their unusually stiff seating arrangements. "We never liked your mother."

"I know."

"So we were all for not liking you," Archer explained.

"Oh, I see," Kelly said.

"And we definitely didn't want you, you know, getting involved with Fannin, although we could see that he pretty much had his mind set on pursuing you. And Fannin's odd that way. Once he starts something, he tackles it with ferocity," Calhoun stated. "We've got a bounty bull in our pasture that in no-wise needs to be here to do the job. A syringe would have done just fine—"

"Wait," Crockett interrupted. "Let's not tell fifty stories here, okay? The point is, we determined to keep you and Fannin apart."

Kelly's eyes widened. "Well, that's all right."

Archer coughed. "It is?"

"Certainly. Fannin and I are not…an item."

"Oh." Last seemed confused by this. "We thought—"

"That you might be getting a new sister-in-law and mother-in-law you didn't like." Kelly spied an extra boot toe peeking around the corner in the kitchen. Clearly, Fannin had not been aware of his brothers' schemes and he wanted to listen in. "I understand completely."

"You do," Crockett said.

"I do." And that pairing of words brought Mimi's warning about the one girl who had loved Fannin to mind. "Trust me," she said. "Apology accepted and no hard feelings. But don't worry about it anymore. Fannin and I would never, ever, under any possible circumstances, get *married*.''

''WELL, THAT WENT OVER like a lead balloon,'' Last said after Kelly went back upstairs. ''Trying to do the right thing sucks.''

''And I don't even think she had PMS,'' Archer said. ''She took us not wanting her and her mother in the family pretty calmly.''

''Yeah, that was weird,'' Calhoun agreed. ''Most girls would cry or have histrionics of some type.''

''So much for our Christmas conscience,'' Crockett said. ''That was a dumb idea, Last.''

''It was not! Confession is good for the soul, particularly on Christmas Eve, you know, right before the heavenly birth and all that,'' Last said in defense of himself.

''Speaking of birth, I'm going to ring Mason's cell. Surely he's ready for a dose of painkillers now.'' Navarro dialed up Mason. ''Hey, bro.''

Fannin left his position of stealth to step into the room. None of his brothers noticed him. He was furious that they had conspired against Kelly and him. But he was happy they had tried to do the right thing by being honest.

He wished he hadn't heard Kelly say she and he would never get married. Somehow that seemed to flip his determination switch to a higher level.

''Dude, that doesn't sound good,'' Navarro said.

"It's starting to snow outside. The flakes aren't big, but the roads may get weird. If you think her contractions are three minutes apart, don't you think it's time to hit it, ol' man?"

Navarro listened for a minute, then said, "Well, we'll all be here. Call us."

He hung up, looking around the room. "Mimi won't go to the hospital, and Mason agrees with her. He should be visited by the men in white coats."

"So now what?" Fannin demanded.

"Mason thinks Mimi might change her mind when the contractions get to about two minutes apart. He says he's lost a pound from sweating, and she's about torn his fingers down to his knuckles."

"Does he want us over there?"

"He specifically said none of us, not even Kelly, are to come near the house. He said Mimi's so wild right now that if she even hears a pin drop, she screams. Helga's got her calm again, but he doesn't want to jinx it."

"Oh, God," Last said, turning pale. "Poor Mason."

They all turned to Last, realizing what had him so spooked. There had been a thirteenth Jefferson brother due—the final one, his mother had promised, she wanted a baker's dozen—but something had gone wrong. Last had found his mother in bed, asleep he thought, but when he couldn't arouse her, he'd run to the fields to get Maverick.

Maverick's beloved wife was gone.

"It's okay, Last," Fannin said. "Don't freak. Someone yell for Kelly. Let's all have a round of schnapps while we wait on the main event."

"I'm going out," Last said.

"On Christmas Eve?" Navarro asked.

"Yeah." Last backed toward the door. "I gotta get...get some air."

Fannin frowned as his little brother left. "I should have seen that coming."

"How could you?" Crockett demanded. "He's the family philosophe. We count on him to be level-headed."

"And we all know he desperately wants children in this house. But that he's not going to put any here himself. Kelly!" Fannin hollered up the stairs. "You know," he told his brothers, "as soon as Christmas is over, I'm starting a serious new search for Maverick. There's some new databases we can check. New technology. And I've even thought about putting Hawk on the job."

Hawk was an amazing tracker. They didn't know much about him, but he'd performed Native-American marriage ceremonies for Ranger and then Tex. He was a pretty cool dude as far as the brothers were concerned.

"Hawk might have some ideas," Crockett said. "Why didn't I think of that?"

"Because none of us wants to be disappointed again," Calhoun said, "and it's Christmas so we're getting frickin' maudlin."

"You bellowed?" Kelly asked, entering the room.

Fannin waved a bottle at her. "Join us for schnapps."

"I think I'd better keep a clear head in case Mama needs me," Kelly said. "Maybe some hot cocoa."

The men all stared at her. Fannin set the bottle down. "Cocoa," he said slowly, "is what we all need."

"I could make us some," Kelly offered.

"I'll help you," Fannin said, walking toward her.

Kelly scooted into the kitchen before Fannin could reach her side. The look in his eye had unnerved her. Busily, she set the kettle on the stove, not surprised when his big hand covered hers.

"Merry Christmas, Kelly," he said.

"Same to you," she said, forcing herself to look up at him.

"Sorry you're having to delay your plans."

She hesitated. But the brothers' earnest apology had touched her heart, and she decided on some honesty of her own. "I don't think I mind, exactly."

Fannin grinned down at her. "Maybe you and I could start over. I've been pretty hard on you. My brothers aren't the only ones who owe you an apology. I've shown you my worst side."

"Oh. Are you trying to tell me that wasn't the real you?"

"It was the real me trying to catch you without acting like I was," he explained.

"And now you want to be up-front about it?"

"Honesty. That's my new policy."

"I see." Kelly thought about Mimi and Mason and unrequited love. And children growing up with single parents—it was something the Jeffersons, Mimi and she all had in common—and then she shook her head. "I'm so sorry, Fannin. It just wouldn't work."

"Because?"

"Because I'm pretty sure you were right. You're that fling I never had. The one before I find Mr. Right. And I'm pretty sure I'm just a fling for you. It would fit your pattern, according to Mimi."

"Mimi? Mimi doesn't know anything."

"I bet she does." Kelly turned the stove on. "How's Princess and Bloodthirsty Black, by the way?"

"Chillin' and not willin'. I'm taking Bloodthirsty back this week. I guess he's not Princess's type. I'm going to have to get her pregnant the easy, one-shot-does-it-all way."

Kelly smiled sadly. "Fannin, whether you know it or not, you're a family man. You're a man of the land, *this* land. And that's a good thing. But I don't want children right now. I'm not brave or unselfish like Mimi."

"Mimi is selfish like Scarlett O'Hara. She's just cute about it."

Kelly shook her head. "What I really want is to go live in my father's world, in the house he left me, so that I can put together the missing parts of *me*."

Fannin pulled away from Kelly slowly, the light in

his eyes fading. "I understand. Believe me, I understand better than you know."

"Fannin—"

He held up a hand, backing out of the kitchen. "You know, I think I'll have that schnapps after all."

His brothers heard him and huzzahed for schnapps, but they had no idea they were drinking to the end of his love affair.

His determined switch for Kelly had flipped to Off.

Chapter Twelve

In the Cannady house, Mimi let out one last determined yell, and before Mason knew it, he was holding a handful of slippery baby. "Oh, Lord," he said reverently. "Mimi! You did it! Look!"

Mimi looked up, her face shining with love and pride. "It's a girl," she said with delight. "Daddy, did you hear that? It's a girl!"

"I've got me another little lady," her father called. "Merry Christmas, Mimi, honey."

Mimi smiled at Mason through teary eyes. "I felt my daddy praying for me. I barely had any pain... His prayers washed over me like beautiful waves. It was the most miraculous thing that I've ever felt."

Mason smiled at her. It was Christmas morning now, with early-morning light filtering through the frilly curtains in Mimi's room. Mason grinned as Helga took the baby from him and put it on Mimi's stomach.

"Aren't you supposed to spank it?" Mason asked

worriedly. "Hang it upside down and give it a whack?"

"Mason!" Mimi stifled a giggle as Helga pressed lightly on her stomach. "Helga aspirated the baby. She's fine."

"I'll say. Listen to her cry! She's going to be an opera singer!" Mason said proudly. "We'll let her call the cows home. Or she could become an auctioneer."

"I'm going to name her Nanette," Mimi said.

That was as far away from her mother's name as she could get, and Mason had figured on that. "Nanette's a beautiful name, Mimi, honey. I couldn't be prouder if she was my own daughter."

Mimi closed her eyes, lying back against the pillow. Five minutes later Helga had the baby wrapped. She handed Nanette to Mason and indicated that he should take the baby down the hall to Grandpa. "Wait," Mimi said.

He saw that Mimi was going to get up, and he moved quickly to her side. "Mimi, you're scaring me."

"There are some things more scary than a pregnant woman," Mimi told him. "Helga's fixed me up, so I'm fine. And I'm gonna see my daddy's face when he sees his grandchild for the first time."

"Oh, God. I had to pick the most stubborn woman on the planet."

They both overlooked his slip as they moved

slowly to the door like they were bonded at the hip. "I just don't think you should, Mimi."

"Mason," Mimi said impatiently, "in some countries, I'd be going back to work now. I'm not the first woman to get on my feet after having a baby, and I won't be the last. We're only going across the hall, and I don't have enough energy to argue with you. Just get me there, if you have to carry me. Please?"

She looked up at him with those big beautiful eyes he'd always loved, the long plait of blond hair slung over her shoulder, that devilish personality that had always lured him. He loved her. He always had and he always would. There was just no other woman like her.

His heart did not beat without her.

"C'mon, slowpoke," he said. "We're only going a few feet. Pick up the pace."

"Mason, you ass," Mimi said, using her favorite name for him.

"That's right. One foot in front of the other. I've seen ants carry more on their little bodies than you've got on your big strong one, and they move faster."

She ground her teeth, and he heard it, his heart bleeding for her. "Let me carry you," he said.

"No. I'm fine. Just keep talking to me."

"Did I tell you you were beautiful when you gave birth? Like a madonna."

"I was not a madonna, and I told you not to look under the sheet," Mimi said. "You never listen."

"All good running backs look at the ball they're supposed to be catching. What if they drop it?"

They moved into the hallway. "Nanette would have landed on nice soft sheets."

"But she landed in my nice, scrubbed hands instead. And she said, 'Thank you, Uncle Mason.' Didn't you hear her?"

They were on the threshold of Sheriff Cannady's room now, and Mason gently gave Mimi the baby.

"Dad," she said, "I've brought you your granddaughter."

The sheriff reached out his arms.

Mason helped Mimi walk to the bedside and lay the baby inside Sheriff Cannady's arms, against the big man the whole town of Union Junction had relied on for many years.

"I love you, Daddy," Mimi said. "I present you with Nanette Marie Cannady."

The sheriff looked down at his grandchild with tears in his eyes. Then he looked up at Mimi. "I love you, sugar. I lived to enjoy this moment."

"I know. You're going to have lots more, Daddy. Someone's going to have to teach Nanette how to fish."

He smiled. "I'll do that."

Mason put his arm around Mimi to support her as she leaned down to kiss her father.

And Mason realized that he had never had a better Christmas, thanks to this little gal tucked under his arm. She'd driven him insane over the years; she'd gotten him in trouble; she'd made him madder than bees in a shook hive.

But now little Nanette was going to settle Mimi into gentle motherhood. He looked forward to seeing that change of pace. Maybe it was because he was getting older, but that settling thing held a lot of allure for him. And he could watch it all from his easy chair across the pasture.

Except when he was teaching Nanette how to throw footballs and bag deer.

"Dad," Mimi said softly, "I just want you to know I've made a decision. I know having to give up being sheriff has weighed on you. But you don't have to worry anymore." She took a deep breath. "I know you don't like your deputy, though he's been filling in fine. I've been putting together some campaign ideas, and I've decided to run for your spot in the spring."

The sheriff chuckled. "That's my girl."

Mimi smiled. "You just concentrate on getting well."

"You'll make a wonderful sheriff. Maybe the best this town has ever seen," her father said.

"Oh, no," Mason groaned.

FANNIN JUMPED when his cell phone rang while he was taking a breather out by the fence two hours after the baby's birth. All the excitement over Mimi's baby had him tense for some reason. Maybe because Kelly would be leaving soon.

"Hello, sexy cowboy," Lily said. "Santa's on her way."

"Where are you?"

"At the end of the drive. I didn't figure you wanted us pulling up to the house with all your goodies. Man, did I set you back about a year."

He grimaced. "You have always been thorough."

She laughed. "You got it. Come meet us."

He hopped in his truck and drove to meet them. There were so many packages in the back of Lily's truck he thought she must have bought the whole store.

"And I had everything wrapped," Lily told him, "and tagged. I didn't figure you had time."

"I know." He thought about Kelly on the floor in Frisco Joe's old room wrapping so sweetly. "I hate to wrap."

"Most men do. Now you will see that each gift has a tag with someone's name on it. You can write the appropriate message." Lily grinned at him. "And I got something very special for your ladyfriend. But I'm not telling you what it is. I want it to be a surprise."

"Uh, that might be off."

She winked at him. "Not after she sees this. You know, you Jefferson boys are pretty spooky. A girl's gotta watch herself. It's no fun falling head over heels if there's no one there to catch you."

"Hmm." He'd think about that later. "Let's get

this loaded into my truck, Mrs. Claus. I owe you big time.''

"Yes. You do. And we'll eventually collect. Merry Christmas, Fannin.''

He just wished he could say it was.

In Lonely Hearts Station, Last was making a royal pain in the ass of himself. But sometimes even the family philosophe could lose his path.

He'd headed straight for where bad girls could easily be found—the Never Lonely Cut-n-Gurls Salon. He wanted a bad girl to make him forget bad things— and the first bad girl he laid eyes on was the receptionist.

"Hey, cowboy," she said, her voice a curvaceously lilting coo.

"Hey." He squinted at the name tag on the desk. "Valentine.''

She looked him over, his condition clear. "Aren't you one of those wild Jefferson cowboys?''

"Yeah." He liked the sound of that.

"How come you're not over at Delilah's salon?''

"Maybe I'm looking for more than a trim.''

She giggled. "Well then, maybe you've come to the right place, cowboy. Lookee what I've got. This, and a full hot tub of bubbles." She pulled a bottle of Madame Mystery's Mystical Mood Magic from under the counter. "Illegal, seductive and made for a man like you.''

Last grinned. "Is that gonna put me in the mood, sweetheart?"

Valentine smiled and stood, letting one strap fall from her shoulder. "Honey, it's gonna put you in a mood you ain't *never* been in before."

KELLY WENT INTO the back bedroom of Mimi's house, where her mother was resting. "Hey, Mama," Kelly said. "Mimi says she couldn't have done that without you. You were like an angel."

Helga smiled as Kelly sat on the bed next to her. "It was beautiful. Just like when you were born."

They held hands, which were the same down to the fingernails. "Mama," Kelly said, "I'm going to go home now, to Diamond. I'd really like us to have Christmas together in the house. Are you ready to go, or would you rather leave tomorrow?"

"I want to go home," Helga said. "I have been homesick for so long."

"I know. That's why I came here in the first place." To kick some wily Jefferson cowboys into shape and protect her mother from their disrespect. She had succeeded, she thought, based on the apology she'd received from the brothers.

It was unfortunate that she'd lost a piece of her heart in the process.

Only a piece, though. Maybe a chunk. But nothing that wouldn't heal.

"I felt better once you were here," Helga told her.

"I just needed to see you, and though I wish to see my house, I think I'm okay now."

"You need a vacation," Kelly told her.

"Mimi needs me."

Sadness began to fill Kelly. "I know. But Mama, I think…we need to spend some time together. You know I'm going to go to Ireland, probably in the spring. It'll be our last Christmas together in our house for a while."

"No," Helga said, shaking her head. "Do not go to Ireland."

"Mama," Kelly whispered. "I must."

Helga closed her eyes.

"We've done enough for these families. Just a little time for us," Kelly pleaded. "Now that the Honey-Do Agency has gotten more clients, I'm making enough money for you to be able to take some time off and spend it in your home. The way we always wanted. Before, you had to work so hard because you had me to feed and raise. Think of all the times we went without. Now you don't have to."

"I know." Helga looked at her. "But I can't leave Mimi with a new baby and her father to take care of."

Kelly smiled. "I knew you were going to say that."

"Stay here with me."

"Oh, Mama…I can't do that. My job is in Diamond, and our house and my life…"

"Fannin is here."

"Yeah, but—" She looked at her mother's bright

eyes. "No. He's not the man for me. He's pigheaded and bossy, and we'd fight all the time. He wants a little cheerleader to cook him hot meals in the morning and smile as she stirs hot dinners at night. Someone who loves ironing his jeans and..." Her voice trailed off. "I really want a partner, Mama. Someone who doesn't expect me to be their whole world. A man who doesn't want to tell me how he wants it to be."

"I know." Helga grinned. "Those are some stubborn boys. It comes from lacking a mother's touch."

"They're going to go insane when they see all your Christmas presents."

"I have one for you, too. Reach into that drawer and bring me the box that you see there."

Kelly opened the drawer, pulling out a plain brown wooden box with a carved shamrock in the lid.

"Open it," Helga said.

Kelly slowly opened the box, gasping when she saw the gold charm bracelet inside. "It's beautiful!"

"A telephone, because you're always on the phone. A heart, because you are mine," Helga said. "A beer stein from Germany because that's my home. A shamrock from Ireland because I knew you were going to go to your father's home."

"I wish you'd come, too. You like Ireland."

"I liked it when I was there. I just didn't like your father."

Kelly smiled. "You see why I have to be very careful when I finally choose my husband."

Helga patted her hand. "One day you're going to give me grandbabies. Then I will move to wherever you are. Except Ireland."

"You just want me to like Fannin because I'd be close by all the time!" Kelly guessed.

"Well, is it wrong for a mother to want her daughter nearby?"

"You don't even like him."

"No," Helga said with a twinkle in her eyes, "but I do if you do."

"Well, I don't," Kelly assured her…and herself. "But it scares me that you might be thawing."

Helga laughed.

LATE CHRISTMAS EVE, when the rest of the family was at church, Last dragged himself home in a taxi all the way from Lonely Hearts Station. "Here, kitty, kitty, kitty," he called to Bloodthirsty Black after the taxi had left. He received a vicious snort in reply. "Whoo. I might decide to ride you," Last said, approaching the rail. "You look like you need a riding to school you in good manners."

Bloodthirsty eyed the drunken scarecrow in the darkness.

"Hey," Last told him, "did you just call me a scarecrow? I'm pretty sure your mom would be angry if she knew you were calling names. What's that other kitty doing over there?"

Princess ignored them both. Bloodthirsty fixed his horns in Last's direction.

"You know, you shouldn't play like that. Someone might get hurt." He pulled a bottle from his pocket, the Madame Mystery's Mystical Mood Magic that he and Vixen had shared. Vixen? Or was it Comet? Prancer? Cupid? "I don't know, kitty. Ask me next time. Have you seen Santa in the sky net? Net? N-n-yet?" he slurred.

He set the bottle on the post. "Ah. *That* is nectar of the gods. Don't know why I never had any of that before. Guess I was too busy being good all my life."

He winked at Bloodthirsty, or at least he thought he did. The bull backed up, took aim and ran at Last. He rammed the post, but it knocked Last over from sheer force. "Now, kitty," he said as he lay flat on his back looking up at the stars, "that wasn't very nish."

The bottle of Madame Mystery's Mystical Mood Magic fell off the post, dribbling its contents down the post and onto the ground. Bloodthirsty Black snorted, then his nostrils flared. The scent of downed cowboy was not as tempting as the sweet flavor he smelled nearby. His tongue lolled out to lick the post and then the spill on the grass.

"GREAT GOSH-A-MIGHTY!" Archer went running into the kitchen where his brothers sat pondering freshly burned toast and leftover peas from last night's dinner. Mason had spent the night at Mimi's, so it was just the younger brothers for this lonely Christmas breakfast. Sometime in the night, Santa had arrived with a vengeance, leaving so many gaily wrapped packages around Kelly's little red-ribboned tree that all they could do was stare with amazed fear. It was overkill for men who expected switches in their stockings if they got anything at all.

But Archer wasn't concerned with gifts. He flailed his arms. "Last is lying on the ground, and Bloodthirsty Black is all over Princess like stink on sh— cow manure!"

Fannin jumped to his feet along with all his brothers. They ran for the pasture. Fannin couldn't decide if he was more shocked by Last on the ground, lights out, or Bloodthirsty making it with Princess all over the front forty.

Princess seemed very willing, too.

"Guess she wanted to be stormed," Calhoun said to Fannin.

"I'll say. Let's get Mr. Green Jeans up off the grass. Hey, Last, you look like you've been rolling on the ground all night. Only Helga will be able to get the stains out of your pants. And what the *hell* perfume are you covered in?"

They hung Last between them like a flapping shirt on a clothesline and walked him toward the main house.

"I always knew that when the baby decided to sin, it was going to be maximum output," Archer opined.

"Whatever," Fannin said. "He smells like he's been in a house of ill repute. That is some skanky perfume he's wearing."

"Did you see this?" Crockett asked, jogging up to catch them. "Check out this bottle."

Fannin halted, taking his free hand to examine and smell the bottle. He read the label and grimaced. "Throw that in a trash can far away from the house. And somebody keep Mason away until I can get the baby of the family cleaned up. Ask Calhoun and Bandera to keep an eye on Princess. The way Bloodthirsty's going at her, I should have a litter of calves. I don't want him to injure her or himself."

"Wonder what fired him up?" Archer asked.

"I have no idea. Maybe he'd had a blockage of something and didn't feel like it. Whatever it was, it's passed now and he's in raring good form. *That's* the bounty bull I saw my brothers get thrown from."

They walked Last up the stairs and tossed him over the side of the bathtub, then heaved him in completely with his clothes still on, his chin lying on his chest. "Some Christmas morning, Last, you idiot," Fannin said. "Could we ever have a normal family, please?"

"No." Archer bent over to turn on the cold water. "We have family, but it's not normal. Mason would freak if he saw Last in this condition. We've got to get him conscious again."

Fannin shook his head. "Cold water should do the trick. I never saw anybody so out before. It's like Spanish fly or something."

"Wonder if bro had himself a little spanish señorita then? Since he's all messed up."

"I hope not." Fannin grimaced. "In his condition,

he couldn't get a condom on if he tried. He'd be missing that target all night.'' Speaking of condoms, he wanted to wish a special someone Merry Christmas. ''Holler when gorgeous either wakes up or drowns. I want to make a quick phone call.''

''Gotcha.'' Archer fixed Last into a sitting position, sat himself on the toilet lid and began to read a *Playboy* mag he pulled out from underneath the sink.

Fannin sighed and went to Frisco Joe's old room to make the phone call. He thought about the last time he'd seen this room—from the outside looking in—and how beautiful Kelly had been, doing the things a woman did.

All he wanted for Christmas was to talk to her.

If she'd talk to him.

But all he got on the line was a ''This number is no longer in service'' recording.

Chapter Thirteen

Bloodthirsty had definitely done the job, Fannin thought two months later as he stared into the pasture at his fat cow. They could say he'd done it out of season, they could say he should have used a syringe, but it didn't matter now. Princess was one contented cow. She was going to give him a wonderful calf for Mimi's baby.

Nanette was too small to know that she was living in a circle of great love. She was a calm baby, but that was probably due to the fact that Mason barely ever put her down. If he did, another brother was waiting for the handoff. In the evening, it seemed that more of them hung around at Mimi's house now. That way they could keep an eye on the sheriff and Mason and the baby—and, though none of them said it out loud, they were pretty much following the stove.

Helga's food might not be their favorite, but neither was what they cooked. The silent pact between them was that they all quit bitching about Helga. It was a lesson well learned after the bounty of Christmas presents she'd surprised them with.

They didn't deserve her—and they'd learned it the hard way.

The only one who wasn't adjusting well to the new scenario was Fannin. He felt awkward around Helga. He would have liked to blame it on the pervert-on-a-ladder incident.

The truth was, every time he looked at her, he wanted to ask where Kelly was. He'd never been able to give her the gifts Lily had picked out—it was nearly Valentine's Day, and the Christmas presents had taken up residence in his closet next to Kelly's thong.

It had all happened too fast. She made him crazy! In his life, out of his life! One minute he wanted her, the next minute he didn't know what he wanted! All he knew was that she'd changed him. He'd gone from caring what his brothers thought to not giving a damn.

Princess was proof they didn't know anything.

He spent all his time now searching databases for Maverick. Anything to keep his mind off Kelly.

The sad thing was that his mind stayed on her, anyway.

Then it hit him, like great sacks of smarts falling on his stupid head.

All he had to do was go visit the Honey-Do Agency in Diamond, Texas! That's how he'd gotten her in the first place. He'd simply placed an order. Not for her, but for the kind of girl he thought he wanted.

This time, he'd be *her* not-made-to-spec order.

KELLY HELD BACK TEARS as she shut off her computer for the day. The Honey-Do Agency was growing at an alarming rate, which meant she was making a lot of money. Enough to bring her mother home to retire comfortably, which Helga wouldn't do now.

Kelly thought that was ironic. She'd gone to the ranch to save her mother but her mother had decided not to be saved.

"I need saving now," she said to Joy. The agency wasn't the only thing that was growing at an alarming rate.

"Hey," a man's voice said, "I'm here to fill an order."

She whipped around. "Fannin!"

He grinned, and her heart skipped too many beats to count. "What are you doing here?"

"I was just passing through and I decided to take a look at the infamous Honey-Do Agency. None of us had ever seen it." He glanced around, then looked straight at her, from her boots to her long hair. "Nice."

Her gaze lowered.

"Are you glad to see me?" he asked.

They hadn't parted on the most reconciled of terms. "I'm always happy to see a previous customer," she hedged. "Of course, Mother's no longer at your place, so I guess you're not a current client."

Joy jumped out of the Coach bag and went to Fannin. He scooped her up instantly. "She remembers me."

So did I, Kelly wanted to say. "How are all of you? The brothers, I mean?"

"Well, Mason's playing at being an uncle and Last is acting odd. Ever since the night Mimi's baby was born, he's been weird." Fannin shrugged. "The place isn't the same without your mother."

"Oh. Well, she seems a lot less homesick now. I guess it worked out for everybody."

"Except us. The boys almost wish she would come back. Kinda funny, huh?"

Kelly didn't say anything.

"Kelly, I'm sorry. I behaved...badly. I don't know what I was thinking. I wasn't expecting you and you caught me off guard and I tried to play it too cool."

She nodded. "I'm sure we both acted out of character at times. It's hard when you don't know each other."

"You look really nice," he said, to cover the awkwardness. "Beautiful, actually."

"They say the glow of pregnancy agrees with even the homeliest of women," Kelly said.

The smile slowly slipped off his face. "Glow of pregnancy?"

She closed her eyes briefly against the news she was still reeling from. "I suppose twins would make a woman glow twice as much."

"Twins?" He staggered to a chair and fell into it. His gaze went to her stomach and back to her face.

"Call me a dunce, but…you're not trying to tell me you're pregnant with twins, are you?"

"Yeah, I am." She winced. "The doctor thinks he hears two heartbeats. I'm hoping it's gas."

"*My* twins? We're talking about my twins?"

She didn't bother with a reply.

"Oh, my God," he said. He stared at her, stunned. Then he leaped straight out of the chair. "Oh, my God! We're going to have to get married right away. Does your mother know? She's going to be so happy! Well, first she's going to be mad as hell at me. I know she doesn't particularly care for me, but I'll work on her and—"

"No, Fannin." Kelly shook her head. "No marriage."

"But…" He looked at her oddly. "Kelly, you're having my children. Probably my sons," he said in a reverent whisper. "The first sons in the family. I never saw myself as a father…but—" His smile was huge as he shrugged. "Hey, I'm babbling! I don't know what to think. My brothers are going to flip when I tell them that not only is Princess expecting but so is—"

"Fannin!"

"Well, I didn't mean you were like Princess or anything, or that I could hold a candle to Bloodthirsty Black. I mean, you shoulda seen 'im in action!"

"Fannin!" Kelly wasn't sure about this reenergized Fannin. It was like he had a motor in his mouth that was disconnected from his brain. "I don't want anybody to know,'' Kelly said. ''I'm sure you understand.''

''Actually, no, I don't.''

She sighed. ''Not right now, anyway. Fannin, maybe you and I could sort this through ourselves without your whole family being involved. They're kind of busybodies.''

''My brothers are busybodies?''

''Yes.'' She said it with determination. ''You know, I took criticism about my mother from you. You can handle a little truth about your brothers.''

He backed up a step. ''Kelly, that's my family you're talking about.''

''And it was my mother you were free to criticize two months ago.''

''Yeah, but your mother was acting under a misapprehension. My brothers are all great guys.''

She raised her brows. ''Continue, please. You're winning points all over the place.''

''Oh, come on, Kelly. Your mother thought I was a pervert. You know exactly what I'm saying.''

''Yes, I think I do. You're right and I'm wrong. Your family is right, and mine is wrong. You're apologizing, but it has a free-wind feel to it. It blows this way, it blows that way, but either way, it blows.'' She put her hands out for Joy to come to her. The tiny poodle did, but she seemed reluctant. ''Traitor,'' she murmured.

''Well, I think even Joy knows that you might be a trace irrational if you're pregnant with twins. That's kind of funny, because there we were worrying and walking on eggshells because we thought you had PMS. And you were pregnant!''

"PMS?'' Her brows knitted together. "You discussed whether or not I had PMS with your brothers?''

"Well, you were acting odd. We just surmised that you might have PMS. I'm glad my brothers brought it up actually, because I'd never heard of…hang on, Preliminary… Moody… Miserable…I think it was moody. Preliminary Moody Something. Hell, I don't know, Kelly! We'd never had it in our house before. So they warned me, and I was real nice to you.''

"Which just proves my point.'' She gestured Fannin to the door. "They're busybodies, and you have a ham warming between your ears. By Valentine's Day, it should be ready for ham rolls.'' She locked the door. "Goodbye, Fannin.''

"Wait!'' He trotted after her to her car. "You can't walk away like that.''

"I don't want to talk about this anymore.''

"I'll hire you,'' Fannin said quickly.

Kelly looked at him. "To do what?''

"To look for my father with me. I'm pretty sure I'm the man I am today because my father left when we were young. I want to find my roots just as much as you want to find yours.''

She put Joy in the car and looked up at him. "Not everyone has the luxury of excuses for their behavior, Fannin.''

He closed his eyes for a moment, and she was somewhat touched that he was trying so hard.

"I'm not giving you an excuse. I'm telling you that hitting our teen years without parents made us all a little dysfunctional. And there may have been some other small things thrown in, which skewed us from *The Brady Bunch* path. I may not like to hear that, but since people call our ranch Malfunction Junction, there may be some truth to it." He took a deep breath. "I just feel that if I'm going to be a father, I'm bloody well going to do it right. And…better than my father was able to."

That did touch her. "I don't know. What if I have girls? You seemed pretty set on boys in there. I found it a trifle insulting."

"You get insulted too easy. You're a very temperamental redhead." He rubbed at his jaw briskly. "I don't care if we have boys, girls or puppies. I want you and me to find middle ground. For starters."

"Can we?"

"You had me frothing at the mouth for you. I'm sure if you try really hard, it'll come back."

She arched a brow at him.

"And if I try really hard, you may not be so possessed of a desire to kick my pants."

"That's the first sensible thing you've said." She nodded. "Come home with me. We'll set some parameters."

"I'm not real keen on parameters," Fannin said.

"But you'll learn to find them useful," she said.

"But I'm sure I'll learn to find them useful," he replied, going to his truck.

Kelly watched him go, the swagger back in his walk. The truth was, she was glad Fannin was here.

"Although I'm sure he's not the man for me," she told Joy. "I mean, I thought I was having a fling. From fling to father." She started the car. "That seems out-of-order, doesn't it?"

FANNIN STARED around the little three-bedroom home that belonged to Kelly and Helga. It was done in comforting golds, browns and shades of paprika red. Green showed up in living plants of varying sizes, and there was a huge black easy chair he knew right away was meant for him. It looked old, well-worn and comfortable.

But he waited for Kelly's signal that he could make himself at home. "Nice place."

"Thanks." She turned on a lamp with a black shade and gold fringe. "Fannin, I realized something on the way over here. We'll be going from overloaded sex appeal to being parents."

"I still think you're sexy. I mean, I'd have sex right now if you wanted."

"That's not what I meant." Kelly looked as if she was trying not to grind her teeth. "We'd be missing some building blocks of a relationship."

"Well, I'm here. Let's start building." Hey, anything she wanted, she was going to get. He was on a mission to be the father he'd lost. Better, even.

"Let me try it this way. You said I was a girl having her first fling so she could say she lived it up before she got married to Mr. Right."

"Hey, lucky me, huh? I'm fulfilling both of those 'parameters.'" He grinned, pleased with himself. "I do like that word after all. It's starting to roll off my tongue."

"You're impossible, Fannin. You turn everything to your advantage."

"That's a product of growing up in a home with twelve brothers and no parents." He patted her stomach. "These kids are gonna know their daddy. I'm going to be at every football game, every wrestling match, every deer bagging—"

"They might be girls," she said impatiently. "Fannin, you don't listen!"

"I was talking about them being girls," he said with surprise. "Girls do everything guys do, sometimes better. Dang, you should see Mimi gut a deer."

"Gut…a deer?" Kelly went totally white.

"Whoa, there. Hang on, Kelly. Don't get upset. She can also gut a fish—"

Kelly went running from the room.

Fannin blinked, hearing the bathroom door slam. "I don't know what I said, but I think I upset her. Gosh, I thought we were over the evil deer problem." He crept to the door, but instead of weeping, he heard what sounded like Last two months ago, when he finally came to and threw up all over the place. "Oh," he said. When there was a break in the action, he tapped lightly on the door.

He got no answer, so he opened it slowly.

Kelly was crouched over the commode, green as anything he'd ever seen.

"Don't come in," she said.

"I'm coming in." He flushed the toilet since she seemed to be hanging on to the lid for dear life. He took a hair doohickey off the tray on the sink and pulled her hair behind her in an ugly but effective ponytail. "A cold compress on the back of your neck should feel good," he said, laying a cloth he'd run under the sink across her skin. "Are you finished?"

"I think so. I'm so embarrassed."

"Well," he said, handing her a Dixie cup full of water to swish out her mouth, "you're a helluva lot more graceful than Last when you hurl, plus you have aim."

He waited until she spit out the water, and when that didn't produce bad results, he lifted her into his arms.

"Fannin, I'm too heavy for you," she said, lolling her head against his shoulder.

"I've carried cows heavier than you," he said.

"I'm going to slap you when I'm stronger," she murmured. "You're not supposed to compare the mother of your children to a cow."

"Let's not talk about animals anymore," he said, laying her down in the back bedroom. He could tell it was hers because Helga had lovingly decorated the room with beautiful lace and pillows and borders and china figurines. "You're going to be a wonderful mother, just like *your* mother," he said, pulling the covers over her after he took off her shoes.

"What are you going to do?"

"I'm gonna go program your remote," he said. "I can tell I'm going to be here awhile. At least until we get matters resolved to my satisfaction."

"*My* satisfaction."

"I think it is your turn." He patted her shoulder. "I'll not program to any hunting shows."

"Thank you," Kelly said. "I don't like those at all."

He grinned. "And no daytime talk shows. I despise those."

"Deal."

"Good. I think that when people reach a point in their relationship that they can give and take over programming the remote, there's a real chance for success in the relationship."

Light, delicate breathing met his words.

Fannin grinned. "You don't know it, but you're mine."

She didn't move.

"Out like a light," he said with a grin.

Chapter Fourteen

When Kelly awakened, she remembered tossing her crackers...and that Fannin had seen everything. "Ugh," she said. "That's not the way I meant to set parameters," she told Joy—only to discover that Joy wasn't lying on the bed in her usual spot. "And I bet I know where you are, little lady."

She combed her hair, brushed her teeth and checked to make certain she was ready to argue with Fannin again. That seemed to be their main mode of communication.

He was asleep in the big easy chair, her dog in his lap and both of them looking fairly mild-mannered.

Until he opened his eyes. Then his gaze lit with fire.

"Hey, sleepyhead," Fannin said.

"Hey." She sat down across from him. "You stole my dog."

"I think she's stolen me."

Kelly smiled. "She's tricky like that. You gotta watch her."

"And her mom." He ran a hand across Joy's back. "Sorry about earlier. I've got a big mouth. I'm used to Mimi, that's for sure. We didn't have to be delicate around her." He frowned. "Or maybe we should have, and none of us knew how."

"It's fine." She really didn't want to talk about that anymore. "Motherhood's a big step."

"It's huge," he agreed.

"I'll never be the mother mine is, no matter how hard I try. And that scares me."

He looked at her. "So be half. It's more than most people ever get. Anyway, don't sell yourself short, and don't get all worried by looking into the future."

"I have to," she said softly. "Fannin, I don't know how to tell you this, but I don't want to get married."

"We can live in sin for a while. Until the neighbors want to run me out of town on a rail. Then you'll have to make an honest man of me."

She shook her head. "I haven't told Mama yet."

He blinked. "Helga doesn't know she's going to be a grandmother?"

"No."

"Any reason you're keeping this a secret?"

Kelly sighed. "I'm unmarried and pregnant by a Jefferson male, which, although she would get over that, I'm not sure I would. I don't want to live on a ranch. I don't want to live with your brothers."

"That's where my job is," he said stiffly.

"Yes, I know. I'm not suggesting you move. I'm simply saying that there are too many reasons I'm not the right woman for you. We're not the kind of people who would have moved naturally past the fling stage.''

"Hmm," he said. "You sound pretty convinced of that.''

She looked at him sadly. "As selfish and immature as this may sound, I don't think I want to move from thongs to maternity panties with you. I'd like to have one fantasy in my life, Fannin. You had me figured out pretty well.''

"I'll have to think of the appropriate solution for that," Fannin mused. "I guess I'd have to convince you that not only was I your fling, I'm your family man, too.''

Kelly wrinkled her nose. "Let's not get hasty.''

"I could live in Union Junction and you could live here. People have commuter marriages all the time. In fact, Mimi and Brian have one…no, that's not what I want.''

"Me, neither," she said swiftly. "I'll be living in Ireland.''

"I hate it when you say that. It reminds me that you're planning a life without me, and you're just not supposed to be that stubborn.''

She reached over and thumped him lightly on the hand.

"Okay," he said. "See, I'm from a small town. I do not dream of moving to Ireland.''

"I know," she said on a giggle. "Which is what makes our dilemma such a dilemma.''

"When I think of Ireland, I think of leprechauns and beer."

That earned him a shrug. "I think of the house my father left me. It's a ring house," she said, already itching to see it. "I cannot wait to see it."

He looked down at Joy. "Are you taking Tiny Red Hot here?"

"I can't. I'm going to leave her with Mama. I'll miss her dreadfully, but I'd have to have her quarantined and she wouldn't like that."

"I can't believe you're leaving your baby behind." He looked at the dog sadly. "If she's abandoning you, I don't stand a prayer."

Kelly sighed.

"When you tell your mother that you're pregnant with twins and you're going to Ireland, she will disown you and come over to the dark side for good," he told her. "She'll adopt us."

"You don't say that with fear anymore."

"I'm dealing. Coping best I can for a man who was pretty set in his ways. You're changing me, Kelly, and I think that's a good thing. Right now, it feels like a stomachache, but I remember when it felt like an ache in another part of my body."

"Maybe you were more ready to settle down than I was. I was one fling away, and you were already flung."

"Probably." He gave her a total once-over. "Hey, are you taking vitamins and stuff? Eating right?"

"I don't eat much yet. And I'm seeing a doctor."

"Good, because Mimi was rather private about her pregnancy. None of us knew what was going on."

"Obviously, if you thought PMS stood for Preliminary whatever."

"What does it stand for?"

"Nothing we need to discuss for another seven or so months."

He sighed. "Kelly, I'll admit I'm slow, but I'm a good man. I'd make you a good husband."

"I know you would." She couldn't help the sadness welling up inside her. "Fannin, believe me, not marrying you is a gift. It's like setting you free to roam wild. You would not like to be married to a woman like me."

"What woman would I want?"

"The one you ordered. I can't stop thinking about that. You'd marry me, and someday resent me because I wasn't your mother's image."

"Well, you're more like my mother than you know. She was so...gentle. However," he said brightly, "I really am not looking for a mother. I don't even want you to cook for me."

"Really? Mr. I-want-everything-Poppin'-Fresh?"

"That's right. I've reformed. I will do the cooking."

She laughed at him. "What's the catch?"

"Kelly Stone, I have a catch for you, but you have to agree to listen to it with an open mind."

Her brows rose.

Fannin held up a hand, certain he was on to something. He had to convince this woman that he was the route to her dreams coming true.

But he had to be very cagey about it.

"I propose that you marry me right now, in three days—time to get the blood tests done—secretly."

"Secretly?"

"Yes. Just me and you and a drive-by wedding."

She blinked with surprise. He thought piquing her wild side was definitely key.

"Then what?"

"We don't tell a soul. Not your mother, not my brothers. We keep everybody out of the equation except the four of us."

"How does that solve anything, Fannin? You'll have a wife and two kids. And I'll be married to my fling and not my Mr. Right. And we'll be living apart."

He patted the chair. "For the short term, I'll be here."

She narrowed her eyes. "I see where you're going with this."

"I'm sure you do, as the manager of the Honey-Do Agency. I'll be the husband you try out for a month. You can order me just like I ordered you."

Kelly stared at him. "I don't think I can fire a husband."

"This husband you can. I've never had to beg a woman to keep me. We'll do it with prenups and everything. In fact, I bet Brian could draw this up for us. I have the funny feeling something's not all what it should be with Brian and Mimi's marriage.''

"I have a feeling you're right," Kelly murmured.

"We draw up papers. We can draw a line down the middle of this house if you want to. But you try me out. Give me a chance. Just me and you. No Mama, no Jefferson boys."

Joy glanced up at him. "You can stay," he told her. She put her head back down and snuggled deeper in his lap.

"You know, we need to tell her about the children," he said. "Have you told her yet? I'm sure she'll be delighted."

Kelly eyed him. "Have I told my *dog* I'm having children? Is that what you're asking me?"

"I think it's important she knows. In fact, I'm going to ask her for your paw in marriage."

Kelly tossed a jelly bean at him from the bowl on the coffee table in front of her. "I can't tell if you're being serious."

"You don't want to be serious. If you were a serious kind of girl, you would have jumped on my proposal. You would have said, 'Yes, Fannin, I would adore to be the mother of your children, to live on your beautiful ranch, cook your meals, clean your clothes and have sex with you at least five days a week.'"

Kelly started laughing.

Fannin grinned. "As it is, I see I'm going to have to say, 'I would adore to be the father of your children, to live in your beautiful dollhouse, cook your meals, clean you up when you hurl and have sex when you're not moody.'''

"And you're signing on for this."

"You're the mother of my twins. I'm a pretty proud papa right now."

She squinted at him. "And when the month is over? Truly no hard feelings?"

Fannin rolled his head on his neck. "I can't talk about the future."

"You're lying like a rug. Fannin, don't think I don't know that you're trying to have your own way here."

"No, I'm really not. I fully understand that you plan to move to Ireland and live in your father's house. I would, too."

"You would."

"Don't squint your eyes at me. I don't even know where my father ended up, but if I did, I damn sure would be there hanging around, checking it out for a while."

"So you do understand," she said softly.

"Yes. Now let's talk about you trying me out for a month."

"I don't think I like it. I'm kinda squeamish. It feels like a marriage of convenience. And I definitely don't want that."

He came and sat next to her on the sofa. "You've heard of trial separations? We're not going to have one of those. This is a trial marriage."

"Trial sets up expectations to fail."

"I think of it more as a taste test. I just really think if you try me, you'll like me. Possibly even love me." He tweaked her nose. "I also know you'll try very, very hard not to. And that will make me crazy. We'll probably argue a little because you'll be so stubborn."

"You think you've got this all worked out, don't you? Beginning, middle and end?"

He kissed her on the lips softly. "Beginning, middle and no end. Right now we're in the middle."

Her resistance was fading, he could tell. "I don't have a wedding ring for you, but I do have your thong and two presents that Lily picked out for you."

"Who's Lily?"

"Jealous already, my sweet?" he whispered in her ear.

"No." She laughed and pushed him away.

"Yes, you are."

"Curiosity is not jealousy."

"Ah, but curiosity shows you care." He grinned at her. "Lily is the manager of the Union Junction Salon. She played Miss Santa Claus for me this Christmas."

Kelly frowned. "And where was I?"

"Probably wrapping packages. Or maybe you'd already left. And then her sleigh arrived."

"Fannin," she said, laughing, "do not try to make me jealous. It's not fair when I'm pregnant."

"I'm not. Let me run to the truck. Hang on."

He came back a second later and handed her three presents. "Merry Christmas, very late."

"Did you ever open Mama's?"

"I wore it until I got a hole in it."

"Fannin. Why are you so hard on sweaters?"

"I don't know." He frowned. "You'll have to have your mom teach you how to repair sweaters."

She sighed.

"I only know what's in this box. Open it first."

"This is an envelope."

"It's a Christmas card, actually." He grinned.

"My thong's in here, isn't it?"

"Yes. I was going to mail it to you in case you wanted it back. I didn't think I'd ever see you again to give it to you in person."

"And I can't wear it now," Kelly said, putting the envelope aside.

"I'm not wearing it for you. I'll do everything else, but not that." He winked at her. "Now, this elongated box is kinda pretty, don't you think?"

She shook it and it rattled. "Bones. Or a chain."

"I'll have to tell Lily not to shop in the house of horrors next time I tell her to go shopping for my ladyfriend."

"Have you ever considered doing your own shopping?"

He grinned. "Do we write that into the contract?"

She opened the gift, gasping when she pulled out a collar for Joy. "Oh, my gosh, how darling! It's got little hanging charms on it, almost like the bracelet

Mama gave me.'' She looked at it more closely. ''Fannin, this dog collar came from a jewelry store.''

''Well, Lily must have known that Joy was a dog among dogs. Let's slip it on her.''

''Wait. These are fourteen-carat gold charms. And the collar is, too. Fannin, this is too expensive.''

''Nothing's too good for my girls. Although next year, I may do my own shopping.''

''I guess you should. It's beautiful!'' She put it around Joy's neck and removed the other collar. ''Thank you. That's more than you should have done.''

''I'm just glad we opened the box. That could have sat in my closet forever.''

''Do you know what's in this box?'' Kelly held it up to her ear, shaking it. ''I hear nothing.''

''Well, it's a small box, about the size of a jeweler's box. I'm guessing it's earrings or something.''

''Let's see if you're right. No peeking.'' Kelly opened the box, holding it away from Fannin's gaze. ''Oh, my gosh,'' she said. ''Oh, my gosh.'' Then she clipped the box shut. ''You *did* know what was in here.''

''I didn't! I promise. What is it?''

''Have you seen a credit card bill yet? Or did Miss Lily Claus give you an accounting?''

''Well, she gave me something, and I just wrote her a check. I had her buy gifts for everyone, so I knew what the grand total was. But she knew she had carte blanche. What is it?'' he demanded.

Slowly, she turned the box to show it to him.

"Wow," he said. "Lily done good."

It was a lovely, oval-cut sapphire, which matched her eyes completely, set inside a gold filigreed pin.

"I like it," he said. "Do you?"

"I love it," she said. "But I can't accept it."

Chapter Fifteen

Kelly didn't own any jewelry this beautiful. It was something a woman would receive from a man who loved her—and whom she loved in return. "Fannin, it's too much."

"I think it's just enough." He took it out of the box and pinned it on her pajama top. "Stunning with those little blue bows."

She looked at him. "You're determined to ignore my hesitations, aren't you?"

"It's a pin. Not that big a deal."

"To me it is. And I mean hesitations about us."

"Have you decided to try me out for a month?" He smiled. "I think I definitely heard warming in your tone."

It was so hard not to give in to him. He was so sincere. What woman wouldn't want this cowboy? And yet her life had changed completely since she'd met him. Things were moving way too fast. "And when we don't stay together past the month and my mother wants to know why we're not married, and I say, well, we *were* married, she's not going to understand.''

He took her face in his hands, framing her with his steady fingers. ''What you're really afraid of is that once you marry me, you will never want to put me back in the dating pond. I will be the best thing that ever happened to you, and you will spend all your days thanking your lucky stars that you married me.''

''You were doing so well there for a second,'' she murmured.

He grinned. ''You like it when I ladle it on thick. The truth is, Kelly, you're scared of liking me too much. And you're scared that it won't work out between us the same way it didn't work out between your mother and father, and that I'll leave you the same way your father left your mother.''

Her heart tightened as he hit a very sensitive, dark place inside her. The little girl who hadn't understood why Daddy never came back, never came to see her, never wrote. ''I don't think I know how to fit a man into my world. I just can't see it,'' she murmured.

''I know. Believe me, you and I, we are the same person.'' And then he carried her back into her bedroom.

Kelly held her breath as Fannin stripped off his clothes. She watched every smooth muscle flex, every hard part of his body call to her. When he got into bed and merely held her against his chest, she wanted to cry.

Tears of relief.

THE RINGING of his cell phone pulled Fannin from a sound sleep. Gently moving himself from Kelly's arms, he got out of bed and left the room so he wouldn't wake her. "It's Fannin," he said.

"Fannin, dude, you're going to have to come home," Last said.

Fannin frowned as he stared out the window into Kelly's yard. By daylight, the yard seemed much smaller, more compact. Compared to looking out at his ranch's vista, it was strange. "What's up?"

"You're not going to believe this, but—" Last's voice trembled "—Mason's gone."

"Where did he go? Store? Cattle auction?"

"No, he's *gone*. As in left. Hit the road. We are triple-O."

When they were younger, the boys had idealized 007, the spy who could solve any problem. They'd come up with triple-O for their alias, short for "on our own." It was strange that Last had brought it up now and forced Fannin to pay closer attention to Last's current rambling. "Last, calm down. It's going to be all right. There's an explanation. Mason wouldn't desert the ranch and Mimi and his new niece—"

"He did. There's a note here saying—" Last choked back tears in his voice "—the note says he's never been away. Never had a vacation. He loves us, but he needs time. Time for what, he doesn't say. How much time, I don't know, either. All he left was this note, Fannin."

Cold chills ran over Fannin. There was no way Mason would just leave the way Maverick had, would he? A note was too cruel. Why not sit the brothers down and tell them?

"I don't understand," Fannin said.

"I think I do." Last blew his nose. "Mason was afraid."

Fannin grunted. Mason was afraid of damn little. "Of what?"

"He…he felt he was having inappropriate feelings for Mimi. And her baby."

Fannin closed his eyes. "Do you know this for a fact, Last, or is this the family philosophe speaking?"

"I feel I'm pretty dead-on about this. He's been spending a lot of time over there, you know, with the baby and all. Heck, all of us have, I mean, Helga's over there."

"Helga?"

"Well," Last said, his tone embarrassed, "she cooks better than any of us. And I think sauerkraut may be growing on us."

Just like a dog, following his bowl. "And so how is this different from how Mimi and Mason always were?"

"I don't know. It's just a hunch I had. It was the way Mason looked at Mimi when she was nursing the baby. And the way he…looked at Mimi, period. He looked like he was in love."

"Big shock, that."

"Yeah, but Mason has never admitted it to himself."

"He wouldn't abandon the ranch over Mimi."

"Not necessarily Mimi. But honor, Fannin, honor. If he realized that he'd fallen in love with another man's wife, that living next door to her was too much temptation and that he was eventually going to make a mistake, yeah, Mason would go. Mason would tear off his hand before he did something he considered wrong. You know that."

"Damn it, I've sort of got my own fire I'm trying to put out," Fannin said with a glance back toward Kelly's bedroom. He hoped she was feeling better. He'd hated seeing her sick. When she awoke, he was going to fix her whatever she wanted—

"Fannin, I wouldn't have called you if it wasn't an emergency," Last said desperately. "We're direly shorthanded. We can't run this ranch with the both of you gone. It leaves just a few of us here. As it is, we're about two ticks shy of having to hire outside help. Or calling home the married brothers."

Neither of those options was workable. Where the hell could Mason have gone? Surely it was simple. Maybe he went into the city for a fast lay, drinks and tears over love gone wrong.

Fannin shook his head. Any of them might live their life to the lyrics of a hurtin' country-western tune, but if Mason had left, it was because his soul was truly tearing.

And they'd all witnessed that before. With Maverick. "I'll be there as quick as I can," Fannin said.

KELLY OPENED HER EYES to see her cowboy staring down at her. "Hey," she said softly.

"Hey." He touched her hair, gently moving it from her face. "You look like a child when you're asleep. No worries."

She rolled onto her side, cushioning her head on her arm so that she could look up at him. "Because you were here. I felt safe, I think."

A shadow crossed his face, and Kelly knew she'd slept through one of those seconds when you were never quite sure what happened, but your life changed. "Have you changed your mind about offering yourself up as a husband sacrifice?"

He smiled. "It's not a sacrifice to be a father."

"Do you wish it hadn't happened?" she asked softly.

"The pregnancy or you?"

"Either."

"I think you were the smartest delivery that ever got made to my house."

She tugged on his shirt. He leaned down to kiss her, warmly, deeply.

"Do you regret it?" he asked.

"I don't think so. I mean, at first I was pretty overwhelmed. Twins scared me. But even if we decide not to do anything more than a trial marriage, I know you intend to be a father to my children and that means a lot to me.''

''Husband and father,'' he said, growling into her neck so that she giggled. ''Unfortunately, I'm going to have to wait on the husband trial.''

A shiver sneaked across her skin. ''What happened?''

''I'm needed at the ranch.''

She blinked at him. ''So we'll start later than we planned, I guess.''

''I don't remember you ever saying yes. All this enthusiasm is good for my heart.''

Only a small smile rose to her lips. Fear was touching her heart. Kelly sat up and walked into the den, deciding that if Fannin was leaving her, she didn't want to be lying in a bed when he told her. ''When will you be back?''

''Not sure. Mason's gone.''

''Gone?''

''I'm sure he's not gone for long. Mason's never left that ranch for more than a couple of weeks for market.''

''Yes, but…'' Mason was the backbone of the ranch. Everybody did their share, but he was the soul. ''I'm so sorry, Fannin. I mean, I know that's not the most appropriate thing to say, because it sounds like he's never coming back, which of course, he will—''

Fannin put a hand over her mouth. She looked up at him, her eyes wide.

"He'll be back," Fannin said, taking his hand down. "He would never abandon our family for good."

"Of course not," Kelly said hurriedly. "Fannin, my God."

"So. The only way this is going to work is if you come back with me, Kelly. Right now. Today."

"I can't do that. My job is here," Kelly said. "I can't just leave Julia in the lurch."

"Then I'll come back and get you this weekend. Be packed and ready."

Her eyes widened. "Fannin, I can't just leave like that."

"I don't think we should waste time telling the family about the babies. Do you?"

"I guess not…" She wasn't ready to tell Helga.

"When were you planning on telling your mother?"

"I don't know. I think I'm still in shock. Having twins is something I have to fit into my life. And I wasn't expecting you to show up yesterday." She took a deep breath. "I really need a little time to get the big picture all figured out."

"Kelly." He put his hands on her shoulders. "We need to figure out the big picture now. I'm leaving. I don't know when I can come back. I'd rather you come with me, because I don't want to sort out details over the phone."

They didn't know each other that well. Phone discussions of the big decisions facing them didn't appeal to her, either. But she was so scared of making the wrong turn with this man. There was so much to think about at one time. ''Fannin,'' she said, her voice soft, ''what about love?''

His hands fell from her shoulders. ''I'm hoping it will come with time.''

She took a deep breath. ''All right.''

''All right, what?''

''All right, next subject.''

He seemed disappointed. She didn't know what else to say. Love mattered for her.

''Come back with me,'' he said huskily.

''Call me crazy, but I don't see how it's beneficial to us to be around your brothers and my mother when we're trying to fall in love. To feel romance. Am I wrong?'' Kelly asked, her tone wondering.

He ran a hand back through his hair. ''You know, I had a cow I wanted impregnated by a bull I felt had great potential and bloodlines. So I brought him in. And I remember my brothers laughing at me as we all stood around watching, and me telling Princess to feel the romance.'' A wry smile touched his lips. ''They told me it would be so much easier with a syringe.''

She knew parts of this story. ''And?''

''I wonder if Princess and Bloodthirsty couldn't get it together because we were standing around watching.''

''It's hard to make love grow when it's under a microscope. I would be so embarrassed. You know, everything's fine between your brothers and me now. They apologized for giving me a hard time." She looked down at her hands. "But I can't say I'd be comfortable being romantic around them. I'd probably feel like I needed to be fixing them meals. You know, to earn my keep. And I'm sure you wouldn't be all that comfortable kissing me around my mother, would you?"

"We might want to wait for that phase of our relationship," he said hastily.

"Well, there we have it. You can watch me throw up with ease, but you wouldn't kiss me in front of my mother."

"I didn't say *wouldn't*," he said, touching the tip of her nose gently, "but I'm pretty sure it would feel strange."

"I'm not coming with you," she said.

"Maybe that's for the best. It goes against my nature, but I...I think maybe you have a point."

She felt tears fill her eyes against her will. "This isn't going to work, is it?"

He wrapped his arms around her. "Yeah. It will."

Kelly closed her eyes, hearing his words—but also hearing the doubt in his tone.

FANNIN WAS HIDING under brave words. He waved goodbye as he left Kelly on the porch of her house. There were no kisses, no tears for their parting. He was so torn in two he didn't know what to think. First, to discover he was going to be a father, and then to realize from Kelly's own lips that she didn't love him. What had she said? What about love?

And he'd said, I'm hoping it comes in time.

He headed his truck down the road. Love didn't come in time. She either loved him or she didn't. Certainly he was in love with her, had been from the moment he laid eyes on her. Why couldn't it be simple?

The truth was, Kelly was right—everything about them was opposite. Different dreams, desires, hopes. He wanted her to come live at the ranch with him, fill in that piece of his comfortable life that was missing.

She wanted him to follow her to Ireland. He blew out a breath. That was not going to happen. While he understood her need to go, he hoped she understood his need to stay where his job was. His brothers had been all about getting off the ranch. All four of them had been delighted to leave Malfunction Junction behind.

He wouldn't feel that way.

But twins.

Somehow, he and Kelly were going to have to…what? Fall in love? Make sacrifices for each other? For the children?

And underneath these raging thoughts was fear. Mason had left, just like Maverick. Maybe not for forever, but he had left. And when your eldest brother, the man you admired most in life, had cashed in his chips and hit the road running, it kinda made a man evaluate just how much caca he was getting himself into.

The worst thing that could happen would be for him and Kelly to make a decision that would make them miserable.

Chapter Sixteen

Two weeks passed agonizingly slowly for Kelly. Every night Fannin called. He was doing the manual labor of three men and making the hard decisions Mason usually made. When Fannin finally got to his room at night to call her, he sounded exhausted.

Kelly wasn't faring a whole lot better. She didn't have morning sickness. She had all-day, minute-to-minute sickness.

Julia was getting worried. "What does the doctor say?"

"That it will pass." She handed Julia a file and wrote down a client's name for an order. "Three to four months into a pregnancy is when it supposedly gets better."

"You seem so thin and tired to me," Julia said. "I really hate that you're working so much. Maybe you need some time off. A change of scenery. A look at Fannin."

Kelly smiled. "Even if I went to Union Junction,

I'd just be in the way. He'd be checking up on me all the time.''

"But still. Are you really going to marry him?''

"I don't think so. To be honest, I think he was trying to do the right thing when he suggested the trial marriage. I'm sure both of us are thinking with clearer heads now.''

"He did send you two dozen red roses for Valentine's Day. One dozen for each baby.''

Kelly nodded. "I'm glad he's happy about the pregnancy.''

"Mimi called me.''

Kelly glanced up. "She did? What did she say?''

"That the baby is adorable, but she's still tired. Her father is happier than she's seen him in years. That if she didn't know better, she'd think he was making some kind of recovery. And that Mason is an ass.''

"Yeah, but she says that every time you talk to her. I knew Mason was an ass before I ever met him. It's her pet name for him.'' Kelly frowned. "Actually, when you meet Mason, you'll see at once that he's the last man you'd ever call an ass.''

"Mimi feels totally betrayed that he left the way he did.'' Julia snapped her fingers. "Just like that. After spending days holding Nanette and taking care of Mimi, the last thing Mimi expected was for him to disappear.''

"Wonder why Mimi doesn't ever talk about Brian?'' Lately it seemed Kelly was possessed of an urge to talk about Fannin all the time. She had to bite her tongue sometimes to not wear poor Julia out with talking about him, wondering what he was doing.

It was actually starting to get on her nerves. His comment about hoping love would come in time had really rankled her. "Love just doesn't grow on a bush," she said grumpily.

"Pardon?" Julia asked.

"I was thinking about Mimi," Kelly said hastily. "And wondering why she doesn't have a pet name for Brian."

Julia put down a stack of papers. "Marriage of convenience. What can I say? I've known my friend for years. I know things about her that only Mason knows, or maybe only suspects. The sheriff, me and Mason are the only people who really know Mimi, and we're just scratching the surface of that woman. The unpretty answer is that Mimi wanted something. She met a man who would give it to her. Now that she's got it, it's the end of that relationship."

Kelly's eyes widened. "Doesn't he want to be around his child?"

"Does he act like he does? Has Brian been in to see Nanette?"

"Only once that I know of. There could have been more times—"

"No." Julia shook her head. "That was a true marriage of convenience. And he's conveniently gotten lost."

"But what did he get out of it?" Kelly couldn't understand the concept.

"You wouldn't believe me if I told you."

Kelly's eyes widened.

"You cannot tell a soul," Julia said. "Though it will come to light eventually."

"I'm not certain I should hear this," Kelly murmured, her curiosity burning all the same.

"Mimi gave Brian a quarter of her property if he married her and she became pregnant. Sex of child didn't matter."

Kelly put down everything she was holding. "No."

Julia nodded. "Yes. Mimi would have sold her soul to have a grandbaby for her father. Whatever she has to do to keep him alive, she will do."

"Does her father know?"

"I think the sheriff suspects about the land and knows the truth about the marriage. But I tell you who it will kill—Mason. He would have bought that property from Mimi. The Jeffersons always saw their properties as intermingled."

"Oh, dear."

"Notice I said Mason would have bought the property. He would not have married Mimi, nor have given her a child. Of course, that's probably no longer true, now that Mason's had the pincers of sense applied to his skull."

"Pincers of sense?"

"Well, I'm no oracle, but I don't think there'll ever be anybody for Mason except Mimi. You know, I'm kind of a believer in the one-true-love theory. We can have many loves, but there's usually only one true love per lifetime. What do you think?'' Julia looked at her curiously.

''I think…'' Kelly said thoughtfully. ''I think I didn't have to give away a quarter of anything and I ended up with two.''

Julia laughed. ''Might be true love.''

''YOU'RE GOING TO BE A FATHER?'' Last asked, gaping at Fannin intently as they all sat around the dinner table at the sheriff's house. Mimi was upstairs nursing, and the brothers had learned to turn their faces away from the stairwell to discuss anything they didn't want the sheriff to be privy to.

But this just burst out of Last's mouth.

Fannin held up a hand, motioning for everybody to turn their heads and talk low. ''Yeah, I am, actually.''

Last nearly jumped up out of his chair. ''That's great news!''

Fannin grunted.

''Are ya gonna be a husband?'' Crockett wanted to know. ''And whose is it?''

''Kelly's,'' Fannin said sternly.

''Oh,'' the brothers chorused.

''But she hasn't been around in a long time,'' Last said, confused. ''Does she like you?''

Fannin pondered Kelly asking him about love. ''We're fond of each other.''

Everybody groaned. ''That doesn't sound promising,'' Calhoun said.

"Mason's gonna kick your butt if you got Helga's little girl pregnant and don't marry her!" Archer said.

"Yeah, and you're going to get the lecture," Last said. "Condoms are our friend. Condoms keep our lovin' from going in the oven. Condoms—"

"That's enough, Last." Fannin tried to tell himself everything was going to be fine, that these were men he loved and not ones he wanted to slap the stupids out of. "I do love Kelly. I fell in love with her when I met her. The lady in question is not convinced she wants to marry me."

"Dude, you didn't play her hard enough." Navarro looked wise. "The less attention you give a woman, the happier she is. The more she'll chase you!"

"You were obviously giving her lots of attention," Last said sadly. "Too much."

"We're having twins," Fannin said.

The brothers were struck dumb for several moments.

"Man," Last said, "you musta got into whatever Bloodthirsty was drinking. Humpty-humpty."

Fannin ground his teeth together. Told himself to remain calm. "You're apes in human apparel."

"We're merely fascinated attendants to your one-act play," Calhoun said. "Pew-sitters in your church of drama."

"Okay, that's it." Fannin stood. "I've got to talk to Helga."

"What for?" Crockett's eyes bugged. "You're not

going to tell her, are you? I'm pretty sure she's bliss-fully ignorant. Have you thought of how she's going to react to the news that you've…you know…had relations with her daughter? And that you're not get-ting married?''

''I didn't say we're not. I said the lady is thinking it through.'' Fannin stared his brothers down.

''Man, you're in heap big wampum,'' Archer said.

Last slapped his hand on the table. ''*Wampum* means money and that's not what you're trying to say, Archer. Now will everybody shut up and let the man speak? He's asking for our help!''

Fannin sighed. ''I have considered that Helga will not be happy. I know Mason will be disappointed that I put the cart before the horse. I can only warn my brothers that the condom in your hand is not neces-sarily your friend.''

They all gasped, brows in their hairlines.

''And it's time for me to make something happen in this relationship. Either Kelly wants to marry me, or she doesn't. I can't even guess as to what that little firecracker would say to me. She's as riddled as Mimi in some ways.''

''I know Mom riddled Dad plenty,'' Archer said longingly.

''I know. So,'' Fannin said with a sigh, ''it's time for me to throw myself on the pyre. I'm going to go ask Helga for her daughter's hand in marriage.''

They all gasped again.

"You know, I think I'll stay around for a while," Last said, gleefully looking up at the ceiling. "I haven't seen fireworks lately!"

FANNIN APPROACHED HELGA as she was folding sheets in the back bedroom. He knocked against the door so that he wouldn't startle her.

She turned around and nodded at him.

"Hi, Helga," he said.

"Hi," she replied.

Sighing, he wondered how to tell someone that they were expecting twins and would be a grandmother before the year was out.

Then he realized that was Kelly's call to make. All he had to do was ask Helga for Kelly's hand in marriage.

"Helga," he said slowly, "I love your daughter."

She looked at him with bird-bright blue eyes.

"She doesn't love me, but I'm hoping she will one day."

Helga watched him as she folded towels. He wondered how they proposed in Germany, and if it mattered. "Helga, I'd like to ask Kelly to marry me. So…" He took a deep breath. "I'm asking your permission to marry your daughter."

"YOU SAID WHAT TO MAMA?" Kelly exclaimed.

"I asked her if I could ask you to marry me," Fannin said.

"Oh, no, you didn't," Kelly said. "Fannin, you already asked me. We agreed on a trial marriage that we would discuss at a later date. Which I've been meaning to speak with you about but—''

"Kelly, I had to be respectful of your mother.''

"Yes, but…'' Kelly closed her eyes. "Oh, Fannin. I wish you'd told me you were going to do that. What did she say?''

"Well, it was the oddest thing. She didn't say anything. She just looked at me. So I left.''

Kelly sighed. "I'm so sorry. That's really sweet, Fannin.''

"I actually don't see why this conversation has been so difficult. You're pregnant. We're getting married.''

Kelly sobered. "I'd called her yesterday morning and told her about the babies.''

"You did? She doesn't seem unhappy.''

"She's not! She's thrilled. I just didn't tell her you were the father.''

"What?''

"Well,'' Kelly said quickly, "I figured one shocking piece of news at a time! I mean, did you tell your brothers everything at once?''

"Yes, I did.''

"Oh, that's right. You all share everything, including whether or not a girl's got PMS. Mama and I don't gossip over everything. I know our relationship might not seem close, but it is. We just talk about things differently than you do. I guess you'd call it one step at a time.''

"Still, I'm sure she put one and one together and

came up with twins, Kelly. Obviously, if I was asking to marry you, I'm the father.''

"Fannin," Kelly said slowly, "I'm taking a leaf out of Mimi's book."

"What in the hell is that supposed to mean?"

She took a deep breath. "I don't want a trial marriage. I don't want to play around with my life. For you Jeffersons, many times a woman is merely sport. When I asked you about love, you said you hoped it would grow. I don't think that happens exactly. I don't know if people move from fling to final in a couple months. We're going to live half a world away from each other. I just don't think that's the way for children to grow up."

"So where is this going?"

"I've decided to marry an old family friend, Fannin. I want security and a stable home for my children. It's the son of a man who was friends with my mother and my father. He lives in Ireland, near the ring house I inherited. In fact, he's been keeping an eye on it for me."

"I see," Fannin said coldly.

"You probably don't see now," Kelly said, "but Fannin, I think you will, when you think this through!"

"No, I don't think I will," he said, and then she heard the phone click.

FANNIN WAS SO MAD he thought his head was going to pop off his shoulders. That little girl was yanking his chain, and he didn't like it one bit! "She's crazy," he muttered.

"What's that?" Mimi asked, passing him in the kitchen to get fresh water for the baby's bathtub.

Turning, he said, "Mimi, you're about the craziest gal I've ever known."

"Thank you, Fannin. I love you, too." Blissfully ignoring him, she filled the tiny bathtub. "Nanette's getting to be such a big girl."

"Yes, yes, I know. Mimi, I need you to give me some—what do my brothers call it?—chick stuff."

She stared at him. "What are you talking about?"

"I need to get inside a woman's head."

"Never. Trust me. That is a movie theater in which no man really wants to run the projector." She turned, then stopped at the look on his face. "Is something wrong?"

"Yes," he said, feeling pressure in his back molars from the feelings he was trying to contain. "I need a woman's opinion."

"Well, why didn't you say so?" She sat down at the kitchen table.

"I did."

"No, you said something silly about chick stuff. Women like it when a man straight talks them. None of that allegorical nonsense."

He sighed. "Do you remember Kelly, Helga's daughter?"

"Of course. I can't remember what I ate for breakfast yesterday, but I think short-term memory loss is normal for this stage of new motherhood.''

"Mimi, pay attention!"

"I am, Fannin!" she said, annoyed. "Would you just get to the point?"

"Kelly is having twins!" he yelled.

"Twins? As in babies?"

"Yes. Babies, for crying out loud. Two of what you just had."

"Whew. She has my sympathies. And my congratulations." Mimi brightened. "Who's the father?"

"I'm the father!" he hollered, feeling like he was going to have a stroke.

Mimi looked hurt. "Gosh, Fannin, no need to chew my head off. You're going to upset Nanette."

He took a deep breath. "I'm sorry. It's just that nobody seems to think that I have much to do with the fact that Kelly's having babies."

"I'd say you've had a lot to do with it." She frowned at him. "Does Mason know? You're going to get the condom lecture. Condoms are our friends—"

"How do you know about that?" he demanded.

"Oh, my gosh. Like y'all ever kept it a secret. He practically sang it to you boys in lullaby form from the age you started wearing deodorant and discovered your first zit. I thought I heard Last repeating it over and over one day when he was throwing feed out to those chickens we had once. Remember those?"

"I'm not worried about Mason right now," he

interrupted. "I'm worried because Kelly says she's marrying someone else."

Mimi started giggling.

"What in the hell is so funny?"

"All of you Jefferson boys. Your love lives are train wrecks. Just watch 'em derail."

He frowned. "She says she's taking a leaf out of your book."

"And what fine leaf would that be?"

"The one where you marry a man you don't love in order to have a father for your children."

Mimi straightened. "I think I hear Nanette calling me."

"Wait, Mimi." A sigh escaped him. "Look. I love her. I want to be her husband."

"So go do it," Mimi said, supremely annoyed. "Instead of sitting in my kitchen playing 'Cry Me a River' on the tiny-whiny fiddle."

"I—"

"Stop," she said. "If you are saying 'I' because you cannot have it your way, then go away and stop wasting my time. You can laugh all you want about what I did, Fannin, but I knew exactly what I wanted and what I had to do to get it. I am happy with my life now. In fact, it's beatific."

What about Mason, he wanted to say, but her eyes dared him to say a word on that subject.

"So go," Mimi said stubbornly. "Either go and get what you want or go sit in your own house and mope." She got up. "Did you ever notice how you were always telling Kelly what she had to do in order to please you? You listened to what her needs and dreams were, and then you ignored them. You said, Yes, Kelly, I'm not keen on your mother and you're too independent for me, but if you want me, you'll have to do it the way I like it. And no woman with half a brain in her head would want that, Fannin.

"But you found a woman with a full brain inside her skull, so why shouldn't she leave you on the vine for a less intelligent female to pick? And so, we have the continuing saga of the Jefferson male quest for what pleases them." She took a deep breath. "Was that the expertise you needed?"

"I think that should just about do it."

"Felt just like old times, didn't it?" she asked with a wicked smile on her face.

He coughed. "Yeah, somehow it did."

Chapter Seventeen

Matters were never going to be any easier than they were at the ranch, Fannin had decided. Mason had never come home—though they'd had a postcard from Wyoming.

He had figured out that Mason was on a mission to find Maverick. That was fine with him.

Fannin personally didn't have time for any other mission besides the one he was on—a mission to marry the mother of his children, now that Mimi had set him straight.

Quietly he pushed open the door of the Honey-Do Agency. A striking woman looked up at him. "Hi," she said brightly. "Can I help you?"

"I'm Fannin Jefferson."

She nodded. "I'm Julia Finehurst, owner of the Honey-Do Agency. Please come in and make yourself comfortable."

Impossible. But he perched on the edge of a chair, his hat rotating in his fingers.

A red fur-ball came to roost at his feet, brown eyes

staring intently up at him. "Hey, Joy," he said, laying the hat down so he could scoop her up. "Did your mama leave both of us behind? Hey, great necklace, little lady. Looks like I'll have to tell Santa Lily she's a smart girl." He rubbed the little dog's head, gratified by her loyalty.

Dogs were easy. "Maybe I should get a dog," he murmured. "I mean, they still run off, but at least you can put a collar on them."

"What can I do for you, Fannin?" Julia asked, her tone kind.

Fannin tried to relax. He figured Julia knew exactly who he was, so he was blunt. "I'm looking for Kelly."

She nodded. "She's not here, Fannin. I'm sorry."

"Where is she?"

Julia took a deep breath. "Ireland."

He stared, a thousand emotions flooding him at once. Shock and anger choked his good manners. "She can't do that."

"I'm afraid she did." Julia smiled sadly.

He had the feeling she was sad for him. "People do not just get up and move to a different country."

"She has a home there, Fannin. Is it really so surprising, or is it surprising because you didn't want her to do it and she did anyway?"

"Kelly's having my babies. A woman does not desert the father of her children to move to a different continent."

Julia sighed. "You haven't called in a while. You

haven't visited her. The discussion of the trial marriage even died its natural death. The plane ticket was bought months ago, before she even went to Union Junction. What did you want her to do? Throw it all away and hope you'd come around eventually?''

"I've been busy," he growled.

"It was already Kelly's plan before she met you. I told her the best thing she could do was to go find herself. What you and she had didn't seem to be... developing."

He nodded. "I guess you're right." Now what? The woman he loved was gone. "Reckon I'd better go get me a little Irish lass then."

"Not if you plan on going over there and telling her she has to come back here," Julia warned him. "You'll ruin any chance you have of winning Kelly's heart if you go in there with your typical approach. No offense."

His brothers' approach hadn't worked for him at all. *His* approach didn't seem to be working, either. He was willing to listen to this calm, nonjudgmental woman with the sympathetic eyes. "What do you suggest I do? We're having children."

Julia shook her head. "I'm sure you'll figure it out."

"In the meantime, guess I'll buy a plane ticket."

She hesitated. "You'll need a passport. Do you have one?"

"Actually, no."

She got out a pad and a pen. "You can't go anywhere without a passport, I'm afraid. And those take quite a while.''

''How long?''

''Three to six weeks. I can do what I can to help you. We have some experience here with the paperwork, due to some of our clients—''

''I would appreciate any help you can give me.''

''All right.'' She smiled. ''Now we need to discuss how long you plan to stay.''

''I'm not sure.'' Right now, he was making up his plans as he went along. ''I didn't even know Kelly had left the country. Is there a number where I can reach her, by the way?''

Julia wrote a number on a piece of paper, handing it to him silently. ''Maybe you should think about applying for a visa.''

''A visa?''

''In case you decide on an extended stay. More months than weeks, you see.''

''Months? No, I can't leave the ranch for months. I have to…'' He hesitated at the look on Julia's face.

''Maybe a round-trip ticket is more the thing,'' she said lightly. ''Can I look for fares for you, Mr. Jefferson? We provide a full range of services for our clients.''

He had the sudden feeling that he'd been found lacking. ''Thank you.''

Getting up, he put his hat back on and went to the door, struck by a sudden, paralyzing thought. Turning slowly, he said, "You wouldn't know anything about a wedding, would you?"

Julia's expression closed. "I've probably already said more than I should have. I'm sorry."

That was a bad sign. Julia obviously knew that Kelly had mentioned marrying a family friend. He cursed silently to himself.

"You have her phone number," Julia reminded him. "You can ask her any personal details you like."

He nodded.

"And you might also want to leave Joy here," Julia said with a smile.

He hadn't realized he'd nearly carried the dog out the door with him. Her warm body and welcome had given him the strength he needed. "What's going to happen to Joy? Do you need me to take her to Helga for you?"

"For now, she's staying with me. Until I get word on what Kelly plans to do."

"So…" Fannin digested that quickly. "She's not married yet. Or there wouldn't be the possibility of her coming back to get Joy."

"As I said—"

"Thank you," Fannin said happily. "What do you need from me to get the paperwork flowing?"

"I'VE BEEN ENLIGHTENED," Fannin told Kelly over the phone. "I swear, I'm only listening to female tactics from now on. No more men's ideology on handling women. And nothing more from my brothers. That's pretty much a no-brainer.''

He heard Kelly sigh. ''There's nothing wrong with you, Fannin. You just need the right woman. I don't believe I'm her.''

''But would you marry me, anyway? I think I'm more of a long-term convincer than an off-the-cuff romancer. There are benefits to being married to me, I promise. For the long haul.''

She laughed softly, unwillingly. ''Fannin, I have no doubt that you would do the right thing in a flash if I'd let you. But as I said before, I'm not even close to what you ordered that night. You may say it doesn't matter, but it does to me.''

''Put yourself in my place. If you were calling up Dream Boat Bob, how would you describe him? Sean Connery in his younger days?''

''He's still pretty good now,'' Kelly said. ''Technically, if I'd ever ordered a man, he would have been just like you in physical appearance.''

''I'm working on my personality. As fast as I can go,'' Fannin said. ''But there are some fundamental things about me I can't change.''

''Actually, I fell for the whole package,'' Kelly said.

''You did?'' Fannin was shocked. ''So…what's the problem?''

''Your expectations. You would resent me after a while. I don't want to be resented. My parents resented each other totally.''

"Hmm." Long-distance was a tough way to discuss issues like these. He preferred to conquer Kelly with his hands. "I'm not a great conversationalist," he said. "I reason more physically."

"I know. Believe me, it's wonderful. But the thing is, I don't think clearly around you. You totally swept me off my feet. I still can't believe we made it in a truck."

"Hey, that can be a cowboy's fantasy date," he told her. "I'm not picky. I'd have you anywhere I could."

That pulled a giggle from her. "How come you're calling now when it costs you tons, but you stopped calling when I lived in Texas?"

"I don't know. I didn't figure you'd leave," he said honestly. "I thought I had plenty of time to get the ranch under control, and there you'd be, thinking it through like you should."

"Oops for you," she said.

"Yeah. You went off half-cocked and I was mad, and then I thought…I would have done the same thing."

"No, you wouldn't."

"I would. I wish I'd paid better attention so that I could have had a passport and gone with you. Anyway, how are the babies?"

"You are so transparent," she said, "but I almost find your fathering determination admirable. It's really sweet, Fannin. And they're thriving, thanks. They seem to like fresh Irish air, lying on blankets, long walks in the meadow and me not being stressed.''

He moved his jaw as he considered her words. ''Are you getting married?''

''No,'' she said softly. ''I changed my mind about Mimi's leaf. It was a good theory, but then I knew that the only man I would ever really love was you.''

''Then can we please figure out how to make it work?'' Fannin said. ''You're killing me!''

''I don't mean to. Tell you what—you tell me how you see it working and I'll see if I can see it your way. Because so far, I don't.''

''I'll have to think about that,'' he said.

''I thought so,'' she said.

''FANNIN, COULD I TALK to you for a second?'' Last said.

Fannin barely glanced up from the map of Ireland he was poring over in the family library of the main house. ''Shoot.''

''Um, it's…private.''

''Close the door.''

''I mean, it's personal, too.''

Fannin looked up, seeing the distress on his youngest brother's face. He folded the map up. ''I'm listening.'' His mind was on the call he'd had from Julia, telling him his passport was ready. How was that for service? Sure, it had been a while, but he'd talked to Kelly almost every night. They'd learned a lot about each other, filled in a lot of blanks. He was going to recommend Julia and the Honey-Do Agency to everyone he met, out of gratitude for her calm guidance.

"I've got a problem," Last said. "And you're the only one I can talk to about it."

"Sit down." His brother's tone was alarming him. He'd never seen the family philosophe so rattled. "Have you heard from Mason?" It wasn't like Mason to be gone longer than it would take to have a passport made without checking in on the family and, most especially, the baby.

"No. Last credit-card purchase was made in Montana."

"Okay." Fannin mulled that. "He's searching. I'll transfer more money into that account so he can keep moving until he's done." Of course, where Mimi was concerned, he was afraid his brother might never be done.

"I've gotten someone pregnant," Last whispered desperately.

Fannin's eyes went huge, and a rock lodged in his gut. "Are you sure?"

Last nodded. "Yeah, I'm sure."

"Anyone we know, I hope, who's amenable to the idea of marriage?"

Tears slid down Last's face. "She wants to get married this weekend, as soon as we get paperwork and blood tests done. We're supposed to go to Las Vegas to do it fast."

Fannin frowned. "Who is she?"

"Her…her name is Valentine."

Fannin culled his brain looking for a Valentine and came up empty. "Where'd you meet her?"

"The Never Lonely Cut-n-Gurls Salon," Last said miserably. "She's the receptionist. I don't know her last name."

Fannin's jaw sagged. "What were you doing out there?"

A shrug met his question. "I don't know. It was Christmas season, and—"

"I remember." Last had come home zoned, and they'd had to baptize him in cold water. It had literally taken hours for him to ease into a conscious state.

"If I don't marry her or pay her five hundred thousand dollars for her emotional distress, she says she's going to go to the authorities. To sue me."

"Sue for what?" Slow burning flickered in Fannin's gut. That kind of talk was serious.

Last shook his head. "I can't say it."

"Never mind," Fannin said, his whole world bottoming out. "I got the picture."

Two HOURS LATER, Fannin had a game plan. It wasn't a good one, but it was all he had. "Julia," he said, "it's Fannin."

"Hey, Fannin. Ready to do an Irish jig?"

"I'm actually calling to ask you to cancel the plane ticket. We've had something come up at the ranch. And as much as I'd like to go, I can't."

"I see," she said.

"Probably not, but it's something that can't be helped. Thank you for all your help."

"You're welcome," Julia said. "Let me know if there's anything I can do."

"Thanks. But this time there's nothing anyone can do." He hung up and called the brothers in for an emergency conference. Looking them over, he realized this was the moment when he assumed the mantle of guardian for this family. Mason couldn't help them now. No one else had Fannin's desire to hold fast to the ranch and never leave. And that was exactly what had kept him from Kelly. His home was here.

"We have a problem," he told his brothers. "An assault on the good name and financial resources of the Union Junction Ranch. Last, would you care to elaborate?"

His brother broke down sobbing.

Fannin took a deep breath. "I'm not the only one adding to the family. Apparently, Last will be a father, as well."

His brothers stared in shock at the family moral compass, who sat in their father's old wing chair, shaking with fear.

"Never," Calhoun said.

"Condoms are our friend," Archer said.

"Treat ladies with respect," Crockett said. "Wear your condom."

"We expect this from everyone but you, Last," Navarro said.

"Who is she, Fannin?" Bandera wanted to know. "She must be a real looker to catch Last."

His brother's red-rimmed eyes told how miserable he was. Fannin was moved to pity. "Her name is Valentine, and she works at the Never Lonely Cut-n-Gurls Salon."

They stared at Last, their faces scrunched.

"She wants marriage or five hundred thousand dollars for her trouble. Or she goes to the law," Fannin said.

Except for Last's heartbroken gasps, dead silence hung over the room. His head was down on his arms now, and Fannin began to worry for his emotional state.

"For now everybody stays home at night. We bring Helga back to the ranch as a chaperone," Fannin stated. "Mimi's had her for nearly three months. We'll increase her salary so that she can be here, as well."

"Who's going to call Mason?" Archer wondered. "We're going to have to find him now. He'll kill us all if he comes home and finds we've lost that much money."

"Out of the question," Fannin said. "We are neither going to call Mason nor pay this woman that money."

"What are you proposing?" Calhoun wanted to know.

"For now, we call her bluff. She may not be pregnant," Fannin said.

Last's head raised with hope.

"I've got a girlfriend who is, and not only will she not marry me, but she never asked for a dime. All she ever wanted was for me to move to Ireland, which in retrospect sounds like a very small request."

The brothers gasped.

"That would be number five," Crockett said. "Only seven of us left, six if Mason pulls a total Maverick."

"Man, we're in deep doo around here," Navarro moaned. "We are Malfunction Junction for sure."

"I don't think we should be held hostage by a female," Fannin said.

"One of us is always being held hostage," Calhoun said on a groan. "Who are you kidding?"

"I don't know," Fannin said. "Something just isn't ringing true."

Chapter Eighteen

"Fannin," Kelly said urgently. "Fannin."

She stood in his living room, watching him sleep. He looked exhausted. He had what looked like four days' beard growth, and his clothes were wrinkled. His face was gaunt, cheekbones showing beneath dark lids.

He didn't move, so she set Joy and her luggage down. The little dog jumped up in her favorite cowboy's lap, and Fannin instantly woke up. "Hey, little lady," he said to Joy, glancing up suddenly to see Kelly looking down at him. "Hey, big lady!" he said, leaping to his feet to grab her in his arms.

Kelly laughed, knowing she'd done the right thing by coming to the ranch. "Big because of my stomach or big because of my height?"

"You're no teacup poodle," Fannin said, holding her tightly. "What are you doing here?"

"I came to see the father of my children," she said simply. "I needed to see the man I love."

He blinked. "Love?"

"Yeah. Love," she replied.

"But you were in Ireland," he said, and she smiled, running her fingers over his cheeks.

"I was. And Julia called me three days ago and said you'd canceled a trip to Ireland. I was astonished that you'd planned to come at all."

"And so?"

"So I decided to come check on my mother," she said coyly.

"And?"

"And Joy."

"And?"

"And you, cowboy. I figured if you'd bought a plane ticket and still something was keeping you from my side, it must be bad. I want to help you."

"Do you know what happened?"

"I'll confess to calling Mama," Kelly said. "She gave me the rundown." She snuggled underneath his arm so she could stand close to him. "I choose to stand beside you and take care of you while you go through this."

She saw tears in his eyes.

"You're everything I ever wanted in a woman," he told her.

"You're everything I ever wanted in a man."

He nodded, then kissed her deeply. "God, I missed you."

"You won't have to anymore."

"What does that mean?"

"It means," Kelly said slowly, "that I belong with

you. And if that's here at the ranch, then that's where I'll be.''

He put a gentle hand on her stomach. ''I can't ask that of you.''

''You didn't. I ask it of myself.''

''When this is over,'' he said, his tone serious, ''and Mason has returned and everything is normal, you and I are going to live in your ring house. At least six months out of every year.''

She looked up at him, her eyes full of love. ''Once I heard that you'd tried to come to me, I knew that you loved me. Me. That it wasn't just a fling.''

''Yeah. It was,'' Fannin said, ''and I'm going to keep flinging with you until the day I die.''

She giggled. ''I am going to hold you to that promise.'' Then she turned serious. ''What are you going to do about Last's problem?''

''Fight,'' he said. ''That's all we can do. I suppose you realize you'll be marrying me with possible poverty in mind. And maybe a stain on the family name. I'm not joking you. This one's going to be serious.''

''Pfft,'' Kelly said. ''We can take 'em.''

He grinned, the happiest she'd ever seen him. ''I love you,'' he said. ''I always knew you were going to be mine.''

''I love you,'' she said, ''and I wanted you to make me yours.''

''The house is empty,'' he told her. ''We could have a fling before we run to the jewelry store. I can't wait to put my mark on you.''

''Fannin,'' she said, giggling as he carried her up the stairs, ''you're going to hurt something. I'm getting too big for you to carry.''

''Let's find out. Because this feels pretty much like heaven to me.'' He squeezed her bottom as he carried her, and Kelly laughed, completely in love.

This cowboy was made-to-order—for her.

Epilogue

Down by the pond that Tex had beautifully land-
scaped, tiki torches blew gently in the early-evening
breeze. The stylists from Union Junction Salon and
the Lonely Hearts Salon had banded together, string-
ing Tex's trees with tiny white lights and making a
wonderland of the lawn.

Kelly wore a tea-length white gown that her mother
had sprinkled with tiny white seed pearls and sequins,
which twinkled in the firelight. Her hair had been
pulled up high by the Union Junction girls, and beautiful diamond earrings Fannin had chosen dangled
from her ears.

The ring they'd selected together was a stunner.
Two carats of heart-shaped flawless diamond, it was
the loveliest ring Kelly had ever seen.

She looked up at her handsome husband, her heart
beating with happiness. Helga gave her daughter
away, a broad smile on her face. Everything had
worked out just fine between her mother and her new
husband.

She had learned so much in her short time in Ireland. Touching her father's things, walking where he'd walked and living where he'd lived had given her time to forgive the past. He'd had weaknesses, and two of those were his temper and an unforgiving nature. In a letter he'd left her in the family Bible, her father had talked about the disaster pride could wreak in a person's life. You could give up the very things you loved most fighting for your pride.

Kelly had vowed then and there to lance the unhappy memories of her past out of her soul.

And this was the most wonderful night of her life. Kelly touched her stomach where her two babies were growing and thought about the amazing miracle that she was experiencing.

Joy sat at her feet, her attendant. Or maybe Joy was Fannin's attendant. It didn't matter. The little poodle was thrilled to be down by the pond where all the action was.

Mimi came down for a few minutes after the Jefferson men helped her father down from the house in his wheelchair. All the Jefferson brothers who still lived on the ranch were in attendance. And Frisco Joe, Annabelle and Emmie had driven in especially for tonight.

Even Jerry and Delilah from Lonely Hearts Station made it for Fannin's sake. They said only seven more weddings to go—and then the Jefferson boys would be the most married family they'd ever known.

Of course, that brought on some sly, friendly questions as to whether Jerry and Delilah ever intended to tie the knot.

Delilah had simply smiled.

But Kelly knew that strangely wonderful, miraculous things could happen, sometimes when you least expected it. She was sorry about Last's problem and Mimi's predicament and the brothers losing Mason, but she was by Fannin's side now, and she intended to stay there always, for better or worse.

Being with Fannin was a wonderful place to be.

"You're gorgeous," he whispered in her ear.

"I'm wearing the thong that brought us together," she confessed, her smile naughty. "You can look for it tonight. Think about it when you're reaching under my dress to take my garter off."

"Oh, no," Fannin said. "Garter tossing is outlawed for this wedding, my love. No one's ever touching anything of yours except me."

"Whew," Kelly said. "You're making me want to leave my own wedding early and head upstairs."

Fannin grinned. "And one day, my love, I'm going to chase you around Irish fields of green."

She laughed. "And I, my cowboy, will be more than happy to kiss your blarney stone," she said as Fannin pulled her into his arms for a kiss that told her that the happiest beginning of her life was tonight.

*   *   *   *   *

*Turn the page for an excerpt
from Navarro's story,
coming in Fall 2004.
Available only from
Harlequin American Romance.*

Chapter One

Actions speak louder than words. So think your actions over many times.
—Maverick Jefferson when his boys got caught stealing Shoeshine Johnson's bus for a road trip because it was the only vehicle they could all fit into at once

"What has to be done," Navarro Jefferson told his twin, Crockett, as they sat in his truck, "is that one of us goes to live in Lonely Hearts Station. As a sort of mole. To keep an eye on Last's pregnancy matter before it gets further out of hand."

"How would we do that?" Crockett asked. "I think the Never Lonely Cut-n-Gurls would know we were watching their every move."

"All we need to watch is Valentine's," Navarro told his twin. "You and I could swap out, and they'd never know the difference. Tag-team girl-watching."

Crockett blinked. "Why do I find that appealing in

a warped kind of way?" He considered the notion, peering out the truck window toward the Never Lonely Cut-n-Gurls Salon. "Or possibly, I find it depressing. It's been a long time since I've had a woman."

"Whoa," Navarro said. "Too much info."

"Last says he doesn't remember anything about that night except that he was drinking some exceptional firewater."

"Man, I remember every good night I've had with a lady," Navarro bragged. "Even in my dreams."

"More there than not."

Navarro pulled his hat low over his eyes without comment.

"So how do we purge the landscape without raising suspicions? We need to get on the inside," Crockett said.

"Yeah. But bed maneuvers are out. Think we're in enough trouble with this group of ladies."

"Mmm." Crockett studied the goings-on of an attractive band of giggling Never Lonely girls as they left the salon. They were all dressed provocatively, which he appreciated. He wouldn't date any of the girls—not his type—but he certainly appreciated the goodness they were lending to the view. "You could dress in drag and become a stylist alongside them."

"I think not."

"You could become a client."

"I think they'd suspect."

Crockett was silent for a moment. "You could hit on Valentine."

"I'd rather gnaw off my leg. Anyway, that would raise total suspicions."

"Well, then you'd have to prove that your intentions were honest, in order to get the most info out of them. You'd have to get engaged."

Navarro laughed. "Right."

"We could get engaged. If we tag-team spy, we might as well tag-team engage. No one would notice that we were switching out."

"What a novel idea. Why don't we just do something so stupid?"

"I'm serious." Crockett sat straight. "It's not very heroic and it's deceitful, but it would get us on the inside and the info we need to save our bro from Valentine's catch-a-cowboy plot."

"We've done a lot worse, but I don't think Fannin would approve, even in the name of family. And when Mason comes home, he'd roast us for sure."

"I say it's easier to ask forgiveness than get permission."

"I say...you've got a point." Navarro drummed the steering wheel. "How are we going to figure out which of those lovelies we want to sucker?"

"I don't know. How about the little plus-size gal over there with the pretty smile?"

"I think you may be looking at her chest when you talk plus-size. Or the attraction is the fact that we could toss her between us like a doll. She's a little bitty thing, isn't she, all curves and swerves.''

"I dunno. I like blondes," Crockett mused, "and she's not dressed fakey, and she seems kind of cute. Personalitywise, of course. Is there any chance we could reconsider sleeping with our girlfriend?"

"Absolutely not!" Navarro exclaimed.

"Rats. I do tend to fall easily into temptation. I really like a nice ripe bottom on a woman. She looks like she's all peach and no pit."

"She's definitely ripe. Hey, she's coming over! Turn your head and act like you're lost!"

"Hey, guys," the blonde said. "Lost?"

"Yes," Crockett said, because Navarro's face was completely hidden in his hat. "But we want to figure it out ourselves, if you know what I mean."

"Oh. You're adventurous types," she said.

"You could say that," Crockett agreed.

Nina Cakes smiled at the cowboy, realizing at once that here was the answer to her prayers.

"Good," she said. "Because I need a man."

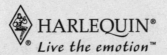

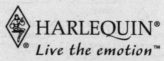

eHARLEQUIN.com

Looking for today's most popular
books at great prices?
At www.eHarlequin.com, we offer:

- An **extensive selection** of romance
  books by top authors!

- **New** releases, Themed Collections
  and hard-to-find **backlist.**

- A sneak peek at Upcoming books.

- Enticing book **excerpts** and **back
  cover copy!**

- Read recommendations from other
  readers (and post your own)!

- Find out what everybody's reading
  in **Bestsellers.**

- **Save BIG** with everyday discounts
  and exclusive online offers!

- Easy, convenient **24-hour shopping.**

- Our **Romance Legend** will help select
  reading that's *exactly* right for you!

**Your purchases are 100%
guarantee—so shop online
at www.eHarlequin.com today!**

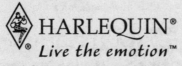

Coming soon from

HARLEQUIN®

AMERICAN *Romance*®

Cowboys
BY
THE DOZEN!

by
TINA LEONARD

The Jefferson brothers of Malfunction Junction,
Texas, know how to lasso a lady's heart—
and then let it go without a ruckus.

But these twelve rowdy ranchers are in for the
ride of their lives when the local ladies begin
rounding up hearts and domesticating
cowboys...by the dozen.

Don't miss—
FRISCO JOE'S FIANCÉE (HAR #977)
available 7/03

LAREDO'S SASSY SWEETHEART (HAR #981)
available 8/03

RANGER'S WILD WOMAN (HAR #986)
available 9/03

TEX TIMES TEN (HAR #989)
available 10/03

Available at your favorite retail outlet.
Only from Harlequin Books!

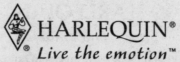

HARLEQUIN®
® *Live the emotion*™

Visit us at www.americanromances.com